SAM CRESCENT

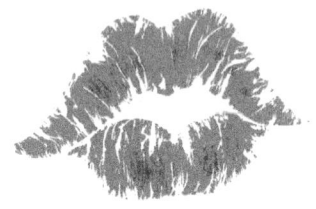

EVERNIGHT PUBLISHING ®

www.evernightpublishing.com

MY KIND OF DIRTY

Copyright© 2018

Sam Crescent

Editor: Karyn White

Cover Artist: Jay Aheer

ISBN: 978-1-77339-709-2

ALL RIGHTS RESERVED

WARNING: The unauthorized reproduction or distribution of this copyrighted work is illegal. No part of this book may be used or reproduced electronically or in print without written permission, except in the case of brief quotations embodied in reviews.

This is a work of fiction. All names, characters, and places are fictitious. Any resemblance to actual events, locales, organizations, or persons, living or dead, is entirely coincidental.

SAM CRESCENT

MY KIND OF DIRTY

Dirty Fuckers MC, 2

Sam Crescent

Copyright © 2016

Chapter One

Drake looked around the clubhouse at the action going on. He loved watching women in different states of arousal. Well, he loved the club sluts who didn't have a problem letting go. There was nothing worse than seeing a woman fighting pleasure, and he'd seen a lot of women do that. Cora and James had left the main part of the club to head to the more private back area. He imagined Caleb and Kitty Cat were already creating a Dom/sub scene.

"What the fuck is wrong?" Leo asked.

The seat on his other side was taken up by Paul.

Both Leo and Paul were known for sharing women, and the last woman they shared, Stacey, hadn't given them the time of day since she had her fun. It made for some awkward moments seeing as Stacey was also Cora's best friend.

Yeah, awkward didn't even begin to cover it.

"Nothing, why?"

"You're sitting here moping. Damn, you've not got another disease again, have you?" Paul asked, pulling away as if he did have a disease.

It had been a long time since Drake got gonorrhea, and it wasn't even his fault. He'd been on the road, and he'd believed some chick who he met in a bar. What-fucking-ever. He was done with women, and their cheating, lying ways. Actually, the club believed he had fucking herpes, but he didn't. After trying to tell them he didn't have herpes, they didn't seem to listen, so he simply stopped trying to tell them the truth.

Throughout his life he'd always ended up with women who either used him to get into the club, or gave him fucking sexually transmitted infections.

"That was a long fucking time ago! And it wasn't fucking herpes!" Drake said, downing his shot of brandy, and relishing the burn as it slid down his throat. He loved the Dirty Fuckers MC, but there were times he really wished they'd get over shit. There was no chance of him ever living shit down, ever. Regardless of whatever infection he had, it was still fucking wrong.

They were his brothers, and they all liked to remind him how damn stupid he could be.

"It's fucking funny that you thought that whore was a virgin. You picked her up in a bar." Leo was kind enough to remind him of the woman who gave him gonorrhea, not herpes as the club all thought.

Before heading to Greater Falls, where they now lived, they'd stopped off at a cowboy bar to have a drink. He'd met a woman while he'd been there—Cindy, which probably wasn't her name. She'd been dressed up like she had gotten out of church, and a whole lot of women had been there with her. They hit it off, and before the end of the night, he had her in his bed, spending the weekend together. Come Monday, he thought he had an old lady, but instead, Cindy turned out to be nothing but a whore who was having one last dirty weekend before she married her very proper husband. Cindy had also been fucking men all over, picking up whatever shit she could get her hands on.

Needless to say, the first chance he got, he had a full workup done, to find that he had gonorrhea, but nothing else.

"Where's Stacey?" he asked, watching them both lose that fucking smile.

"Not cool!" Paul said.

"What? You can talk about the bitches from my past but I can't talk about the bitch from your present?"

After a couple months of fucking, Stacey had stopped going to the club, and was instead dating some teacher, or something like that.

Paul and Leo had left her alone. She was clearly not the one for the two of them. Even though they were not related by blood, Leo and Paul acted like real ass brothers. They also wanted a woman to share between themselves. So far, no one would stick around to be with them.

"We saw her with that prick, Bill at the diner." Leo slammed his hand on the counter, and Jerry who was serving, handed him a bottle of beer. "Fucking bitch is even eating on our fucking turf."

"She didn't want us, Leo. We went in with our eyes open." This came from Paul.

"You can't tell me that you didn't think she was the one?" Leo asked.

Drake sat nursing his shot of brandy, which Jerry had kindly filled up for him.

"Yeah, in the beginning, I did. She could keep up with us, and accepted us as a threesome, but didn't you notice she pretty much ignored us unless she wanted to get off? I'm more than happy to have a bitch suck my dick, and give me all access to her holes, but I'm not going to go fighting a woman for commitment."

"You know what? You two ladies have a lot to work out. I'm going to head into the back, and watch the shows that are about to start. I saw Richard arrive a few minutes ago, and you know how he likes to work the girls over."

Taking his drink, Drake headed toward the back of the clubhouse, entering a secured room, making sure it was closed behind him.

Cora and James were cuddled up in one of the booths, watching the two shows being played out. Caleb had Kitty Cat and was spanking her ass for some imagined wrongdoing. Richard was working a new club whore, Sophie. Richard was balls deep inside of Sophie as he wrapped her hair around his wrist and started to fuck her.

Taking a seat in the booth with James and Cora, Drake saw several of the brothers were watching the show as well.

"What's up?"

"I'm tired of listening to Leo and Paul bitching and moaning about shit." He shrugged.

"They've still got a thing for Stacey," Cora said with a sigh. "I did warn her."

"It's not your problem," James said, stroking his woman's arm.

"What if they blame me?"

"Stacey, Leo, and Paul are all adults. If they didn't want to commit to shit, then that's between them. You didn't make them stick their dicks inside her, and you didn't make her take them. It's between them, keep it there."

Drake sipped at his brandy this time, wondering why he was feeling ... empty. He didn't get it. The club was full of new pussy, even from the town they were currently living, Greater Falls, but he wasn't interested.

"Where's Teri?" he asked.

Teri Davies was their cook, and had taken the diner that they had bought, turning it into one of the places to stop and eat at. The food was out of this world, and had even made some headlines. Teri was also a friend to the club, and occasionally fucked them. Drake had taken a few turns with her, but it hadn't rocked his world.

Glancing over at Cora and James, he was a little envious of the couple. They had found each other when neither of them had actually gone looking. He wasn't some kind of pussy looking for love, but at thirty-nine years old, he was hoping to settle down, maybe even have a couple of kids.

"She's not coming tonight. She's interviewing some woman tomorrow morning who applied for a position as a waitress. Teri wants to be there early enough to see her in action," James said.

"Damn, Teri even said she's making her breakfast casserole tomorrow. I've got to be there for that," Cora said, licking her lips. The woman oozed sex. Even Drake was getting hard, and Cora wasn't his type, not really. She was too feisty, and he liked his women on the gentler side.

"Woman, you're making me hard licking your lips like that."

Cora giggled, running her tongue across her lip slowly. "You thinking about your cock here, baby?"

"Fuck, yeah."

James tugged Cora so that she was straddling his lap, and Drake sighed. He watched as James removed Cora's dress, letting her tits pop out, and lifting it up.

Well, if he was going to get a chance to enjoy the show, he was going to make the most of it. Releasing his cock from the tight confines of his jeans, he started to work from the root down to the base, then back up. He took slow strokes, wanting it to last. The tip was already leaking pre-cum, and he smeared the natural lube into the skin of his cock. Fuck, he wanted a woman to take him into her mouth and suck him down.

His hand was not going to be as good as a woman's tight cunt or mouth, but he'd make do with his hand. At this moment in his life, there was nothing for him to do but take care of business himself.

****

Grace Stewart stared at her reflection in the full length mirror inside the diner's staffroom. Teri had gotten her a uniform that was a perfect fit. The black skirt went down to her knee, and the pumps were comfortable enough that she'd be able to be on her feet all day without being in pain. The crisp, white buttoned shirt was without a single crease, and Teri demanded that she keep it that way every day. She also had a half pinafore at the front, and she had been given a clean pad, plus a pencil for orders. There was also a code for everything on the menu, which changed every single week, depending on Teri's mood, as she was the cook.

There was a knock on the door, and a second later Teri entered.

"Hey, honey, I thought I'd check on you. The doors are open, the food is cooking, and the customers will start to arrive."

Grace looked down at the uniform, and sighed. "Do I look okay?"

"You look beautiful, and nervous. You need to tie your hair back."

She touched her long brown hair and winced. "Shoot, I'm so sorry, I forgot."

"Calm down, Grace. Damn, some bastard did a

number on you."

Grace's cheeks heated at the reminder of what she'd become in the last eight years since leaving Greater Falls for college, and then for a job. She'd told Teri one of the reasons she had come back home. Teri was one of those people she could easily talk to.

"You don't need to keep apologizing. It's your hair, and I'm not going to suddenly bitch at you about it. I've got a spare band. Here, let me." Teri moved behind her, and pulled her hair back into a bun. "You look like a little sex kitten."

"Oh, erm, I don't think—"

"Relax, I'm trying to give you some confidence, honey. You do know that the Dirty Fuckers MC come here to eat, right? They own this diner."

"Yes."

"I'm wanted to make sure that you know it. They wouldn't hurt you, and they won't make you uncomfortable. Obviously some of them will try to get in your pants, but if you tell them no, then no they will listen to."

"Thank you."

"Stop saying thank you. I've not officially given you the job yet. I just hope you know what you're doing." Teri moved toward the door. "Come on, you may as well get stuck in when you can."

Leaving the staffroom, Grace took a deep breath, and entered the main part of the diner. It was a large, family diner, and she'd been surprised to learn a biker club owned it. She always imagined that an MC would have some kind of sex club, or women walking around naked. Too much television in the last couple of weeks hadn't even begun to prepare her for the diner. Teri had warned her that all clubs were different, and this was the way Dirty Fuckers MC rolled.

"Right, you start by filling the pots along the counter, and checking the tables. When people come in, serve them. Chloe's not coming in until after nine, and she'll help you. She's a club girl, so she won't give you any shit. I made sure you were working with some of the nice girls."

"There's not nice girls?" Grace asked.

"Put it this way, some club whores think they have a shot with these men. They need to realize that these men are only after their pussy, nothing else." Teri shrugged. "I guess there would be no drama if they didn't think they were special. I've got to head back into the kitchen. Are you okay?"

"Yes, I think so."

"Oh, there will also be Daniel. He's not long out of high school, and he's wanting to prospect for the club. He'll be waiting with you, but he's a sweetie pie." Teri gave her another beaming smile before walking off.

Okay, filling up the pots of sugar, salt, and ketchup. Teri had already told her where to find the supplies. Grace went into the supply cupboard, getting what she needed and starting to fill the empty containers.

The repetitive action helped to soothe her frayed nerves.

I can do this.

It's simple.

A simple job that doesn't need any kind of instruction or support.

Opening each tub, she filled first the salt, paying careful attention so that she didn't accidentally fill the wrong one.

"Do you really think anyone is going to believe a fat bitch like you? You should be happy that I even want your cellulite riddled ass."

Dwayne's words even though they were in the

past still played through her mind threatening to swallow her whole. She was overweight, and had been when she first met Dwayne in college. At the time she'd been studying business, and instead of finishing her degree, she quit to help him. She'd become one of those women who she screamed at the television to open her eyes to the monster.

In the beginning he'd start by calling her fat, or lard ass, or something more that hurt, but she ignored it. He was her boyfriend, and he said he loved her. It hadn't been long until the name calling had turned to violence. She met Dwayne when she was twenty, and it took her five years until she finally left his cheating, abusive ass. She'd not sneaked away either. Even though she had been petrified, she had packed her bags, to which he laughed, saying she'd be back. Six months later she was back home, and she wondered if he was still laughing.

The sound of the doorbell going had her turning around to find several customers entering. They gave her a smile, and she finished the pot of salt. Wiping her hands, she grabbed the notepad and pencil, walking toward the table. She took the order, promising to be back with coffee.

I can do this.

She placed the order on the roundtable, telling Teri she had an order.

"That wasn't too bad, right?" Teri asked, taking the slip of paper.

"One customer I can handle. Well, two customers." She moved toward the coffeepot. Once the customers had their coffee filled, she moved away to finish her jobs. It wasn't long before the bell started to go off over and over again.

With each new customer, she took a deep breath, and did the job. She was not shy of hard work.

A couple of the customers recognized her, and tried to catch up. Grace was happy to have the excuse of dealing with customers so she didn't have to answer them. Teri kept up with the orders, and she was surprised how smoothly everything ran.

When the bell went again, and she spotted leather clad men, Grace stopped. Looking outside the window she saw several bikes parked there.

Running her hands down her apron, she tried to mentally prepare herself for dealing with the deadly looking bikers. She had imagined them looking greasy and giving out lewd looks to women. The name, Dirty Fuckers, it didn't do them justice, not at all.

They were far from dirty, and as for fuckers, well, she guessed they screwed a lot.

Teri came out of the kitchen and walked over to her.

"Come on, I'll introduce you to the owners of the diner." She took Grace's hand, practically dragging her over to them before she could say anything. "Hey, guys, I'd like you to meet Grace Stewart. She's my newest waitress."

Grace held her hand up. What was she supposed to say?

"That's James and Cora. He's the Prez. There is Pixie, Leo, Paul, Jerry, Drake, Caleb, and oh, Chloe is just pulling up with Kitty Cat. Not all of the guys are here, but I imagine they'll show up at some point. Don't let them scare you."

Teri then moved away as if she hadn't just handed her over to a bunch of wolves.

Holding onto her notepad for dear life, she tried her best to smile at the men. "What can I get you?"

"I know you," Cora said, pointing at her. "You used to live here, right?"

"Yep."

"What happened to your parents?" Cora asked.

Her cheeks heating, Grace held the notebook close to her. "They, erm, they died in a plane crash." It was one of the reasons she'd left town to go to college out of state. She hated the pitying looks, and everyone knowing her business.

"That's right, Stewart, I recognized the name, and of course, you haven't changed much."

Grace smiled. She recognized Cora as well, but she hadn't known much about her. "What do you do now?" Grace asked as it seemed the polite thing to do.

"I'm a secretary at the high school now. Stacey, I think she taught you history?"

"Yes, she did." She remembered. Cora had visited her history teacher.

"It's nice to see you again. Can I get you anything?" *That's it, Grace, remember to serve.*

"The breakfast casserole for me."

Scribbling down Cora's food, she then dealt with the rest of the table's orders before heading toward Teri, who was already waiting.

"Hello, girlfriend, I heard you're the new starter. I'm Chloe."

Grace smiled at the redhead, wishing she could be as open and friendly with the woman.

Thanks, Dwayne, for making me doubt everyone.

"Grace."

"Is there anything you need help with? I'm feeling ready to kick this breakfast's ass. I had such a good workout last night."

"You work out at night? Is that safe?"

Chloe giggled. "I fucked those three men there, baby. That's my way to work out, orgasm all the way."

This wasn't going to be awkward at all!

Chapter Two

Drake watched the young waitress as she moved around the room. He'd not seen her before, but from the sounds of it, she had only just come back from being away. There was sadness in her eyes that intrigued him. She was the only woman so far in his life that had ever tried to fake being happy. He'd never known it before, and it was kind of unusual to him to witness it. Most of the women he saw were always happy for some strange reason, and he didn't know what to make of this woman.

It wasn't an act.

He'd witnessed fear as well, which she tried her hardest to hide.

"See someone you like?" Pixie asked.

Turning toward Pixie, he gave him a pointed look. "Are you going to stop making excuses of buying women's clothes, and ask her out?"

Suzy, a woman who worked at a clothing retail store, had caught Pixie's eye. Since he first saw her, Pixie had used any excuse to go to the store, buying random pieces of crap just to get her attention.

"I'm not after a date."

"You do realize you've got stalker written all over you, right? She could probably get a restraining order or something like that."

"Fuck off, Drake. There's nothing wrong with being thorough when chasing after the woman you want. Besides, I don't want to date her. I want to fuck her."

"Erm, coffee."

Both of them turned to see Grace had returned with the coffeepot. There was a lovely blush to her fine features, and Drake found himself wanting to know more. He liked the sound of her voice. It was sweet, delicate, and the tones sent his cock into overdrive, wanting to get inside her. Fuck! He was getting a damn hard-on from a woman's voice alone. He really needed to do something about the effect this woman was having on him.

Grabbing one of the cups that Teri always left out on their table, he held it for her.

"I take sugar as well, darling."

Even as she poured the hot liquid, he noticed her hand didn't shake. She was embarrassed, but it hadn't taken over her entire body. He liked that.

She reached out, grabbing a white pot. "Here's your sugar." Her attention turned to Pixie. "Can I get you anything?"

"Just pour me some coffee, I'm good to serve myself."

Grace nodded, doing what he wanted, and then leaving.

"Do you really think she's your type?" Pixie asked. "You usually like them to be a little feisty."

"No, *you* like them feisty." He pointed at Cora. When James's woman first visited the clubhouse a year ago, Pixie had tried to set it up so that he and James would share Cora. Once the sharing was done, Pixie would leave, and James would be the one to pick up the shattered mess his brother left behind. Cora had surprised them both. Not only had she told Pixie that she didn't want anything to do with him, she'd then gone and fallen for James.

It had been a long time coming, a woman who preferred the scarred brother as opposed to the cute one with a bad ego. Pixie believed most women wanted to fuck him, so he didn't really have any respect for them.

Drake was rooting for Suzy to keep Pixie away from her. It was about time the brother was taught a lesson that not all women wanted him.

"School is out in three weeks," Cora said. "They're doing their annual graduation fair like last time. Are you all coming?"

"Wouldn't miss it," James said.

"Why the fuck do we have to go?" Leo asked.

"You're part of the town now. It's time you moved on from Stacey. Don't think about her," Cora said.

Speaking of, Drake sighed as he spotted Stacey walking into the diner with her man of the moment.

Great, Leo and Paul looked like they wanted to cause some serious damage. Drake already knew he'd be siding with his friends. When he'd first caught sight of Stacey, he knew she was going to be trouble.

"Cora, can we join you?" Stacey asked, smiling.

Okay, this is just taking it too far. He tensed up waiting for what Cora would say. James, their Prez, had asked them all to give Cora the benefit of the doubt when it came to their friend. Stacey was now rubbing shit in Leo and Paul's face. She knew the two brothers wanted more, and yet, she had fucked them until Bill, the gym teacher had made a move.

"That's not appropriate, Stacey. I suggest you find a table elsewhere," Cora said, surprising him.

There had been a few argued points over the last few months among the brothers because of the friendship between Cora and Stacey.

Leo and Paul had fallen hard for the woman.

"What? Seriously? You're not over that shit yet?" Stacey asked, glaring at both men in question.

Cora stood up, and Drake simply watched.

"Regardless of it they're over you or not, you knew how they felt. You knew they were trying to encourage you to have more with them, to prove to you they could be what you needed. Instead of taking what they had to offer, you waited until fuck-face there was ready to give you the time of day." Cora sneered at Bill. "Misty stop fucking you?"

Bill started to sputter, going red in the face.

"Yeah, I thought so as well. You're still my friend, but I'm part of this club now, Stacey, and you could have been part of that." Cora shrugged. "You picked the wrong guy."

Cora sat down, and Drake watched as Stacey released Bill's hand. She nodded at Cora, and then moved toward the next available table. Grace was at their table within moments, but it looked like Stacey was about to tear him apart.

Drake turned to look at Leo and Paul. They both wore shocked expressions.

"What?" Cora asked as all eyes turned toward her. "You're my family, and even though I'd like Stacey to sit with us, I don't agree with what she did. Besides, it's about time she knew Misty was fucking her man."

"Misty sure gets around," Leo said.

"Don't even think about it. I'll kill that bitch if she ever comes to the club because one of you assholes have invited her. She's a bitch, and I don't like her."

James laughed. "Don't worry about it. Misty is not getting near the club. If the boys want to fuck that whore, they can visit her. From what I hear, there would be a long queue to get to her."

Misty had nearly ruined a marriage between Thomas Redman the local builder, who happened to be friends with the club, and Sharon, the principal of the high school. Thomas hadn't cheated on his wife, but Misty had been spreading rumors, feeding into Sharon's insecurities.

"Here is your order," Grace said, placing down their food.

When she came in close he was sure he smelled strawberries. She left them only to come back seconds later with another set of plates. "Enjoy your breakfast." Another small, forced smile, and then she was gone.

Chloe, the giggling club whore, who also happened to be a nice woman, came toward the table. "She's doing great, don't you think?"

He liked Chloe. She was a real sweetheart and a natural submissive. There had been a time when she had stopped being with Richard, the dark lawyer who visited the club as she felt she was falling in love. What Drake felt really sad over was the fact she had admitted to him that she didn't feel good enough for Richard.

"He's a big time lawyer, you know? He wouldn't even look twice at me."

At the time he'd not said anything. Chloe was one of those women that it was easier to listen to than to console. She twisted words up to suit her, and he noticed there were times she suffered with insecurity. The brothers all adored her. He knew he spoke for all of them when he felt protective of the young woman.

No one would ever hurt their girl, no one.

"Yeah, no freaking out."

"She's not even shaking either. Not very talkative though, but she stares at lot that makes you believe she's listening. Make sense?" Chloe asked.

"Perfect sense," Pixie said, who was staring out of the window.

Wow, this was a day for women who were turning brothers' worlds upside down. Suzy was entering the diner. She didn't stop, but she offered them a smile, moving toward the counter near the kitchen, taking a seat. It was the place where people who were alone sat.

Pixie's gaze was on her, and Drake smiled, winking at Chloe, who giggled once again.

MY KIND OF DIRTY

****

So far, so good. The morning was going great, and she wasn't freaking out even with the Dirty Fuckers in the diner. Teri was encouraging her, along with Chloe. They were lovely women, and she knew that she was going to enjoy working here, if she got the job. Teri was going to make a decision at the end of the day. Grace was stressed as she really wanted the job.

When someone sat at the main counter, she moved behind, and was shocked to discover one of her old friends, Suzy, sitting there.

"Suzy?" Grace said.

"Oh my God, Grace, I heard you were back in town, but I didn't actually know it was true."

Leaning across the counter, Grace wrapped an arm around her old friend. Through college they had both lost touch.

Grace's parents hadn't liked Suzy as she'd been from the wrong side of the tracks.

"How are you?" Grace asked, getting in there first.

"I'm doing great. I'm working at the mall." She mentioned a clothing outlet that Grace recognized. "I'm not living at the trailer anymore. I make my own living, and I have this small two bedroom apartment. What about you?"

"Not a lot to talk about."

"What are you doing back in Greater Falls? I thought you were going to be some hotshot business owner."

Grace smiled. "Things didn't exactly turn out the way that I hoped."

"Where are you staying? I'd love for us to do lunch or dinner, or something. I know you don't like drinking, but I can cook for us."

Grace told Suzy where she was living, in a rundown apartment building, which was the only place she could afford when she first got into town. The last couple of months she had tried to get different jobs, but Greater Falls didn't have many applications so she'd been traveling to the city in the hope of finding a good paying job.

Nothing had come through. A lot of employers didn't like to take a college dropout. She wondered if Dwayne knew she would have struggled to get work, which was why he made her drop out.

"No, I'm not having that. I've got a spare room, and you can come and stay with me," Suzy said.

"What? No, you don't have to do that."

Suzy placed her hand on top of hers. "Don't even think of turning it down. I won't have it. You were the only girl in high school who wasn't hung up on where I lived, and I'm going to show you the same courtesy. We were always friends, Grace."

"I wasn't your friend to get something out of you, Suzy."

"You can pay rent. Come on, it's a good apartment, in a good area, and there's some security as well. It's safe. I wanted safe after years of living in a trailer. Come on, let me do this for you. You were always nice to me."

"You don't have to."

"Please," Suzy said. "We were friends, and to me nothing has changed."

"It has been eight years. How do you know I'm not some addict?"

"This is you, and if you were, the diner wouldn't have hired you. Teri, she's not stupid about that kind of thing. Please, we can catch up."

Grace couldn't think of another excuse to give

her friend, so she agreed. "Sure, why not?"

"I'm working 'til seven tonight. How about I pick you up at your old apartment? Be packed and ready."

"Sure. It sounds like fun."

Moving toward the kitchen, she saw Teri was waiting with a plate. "Suzy called ahead to say that she would be at the diner today. She usually orders out breakfast, and I don't mind taking it to her."

"Okay."

"I'm glad you've taken her up on her offer. It makes no sense fighting your friends." Teri gave her a wink.

The women around her were determined to draw her out of the shell she'd created to protect herself. Putting a plate in front of Suzy, Grace nodded. "Thank you for letting me move in with you. I look forward to it."

"Yay, roommates." Suzy clapped her hands.

"I'm hoping I get the job here though."

"It's okay if you don't. I can wait for the money." Suzy picked up her fork. "I've got work today."

Leaving her friend, Grace spent the rest of the morning until lunchtime going between the tables. Chloe did the same, and they didn't get a lull until around two in the afternoon. The Dirty Fuckers came and went without any trouble.

Teri put a plate of chicken, biscuits, and gravy in front of her. "Eat."

"Oh, okay." She reached into her pocket ready to pay, but Teri held her hand up. "I'm not taking your money, honey. Eat."

Sitting down, she cut up the chicken and took a bite. The meat was so succulent and flavorful. The gravy was so tasty that it made her mouth water for more.

"Teri is one hell of a cook," Chloe said, taking a

seat beside her. Teri came out with two more plates.

Chloe had a large burger, fries, and coleslaw. Teri had the same. They sat and ate.

"So, what's your story?" Chloe asked.

"What?"

"You're an old local, and now you're back. You don't look happy half the time. What gives?" Chloe asked.

"Forgive her, she doesn't have a filter. She doesn't know when to shut the fuck up." Teri gave the other woman a pointed look.

"What? I'm only asking a question."

"You ever thought that it's private?"

"Why the fuck would it be private?" Chloe asked. "We're all girls here."

"It takes time to build up that kind of trust."

Grace looked from one woman to the other, then back again.

"Fine, I like you, Grace," Chloe said.

"Thanks, I think."

Chloe nodded, and the smile was back on her face. "Did you see Stacey snapping at Bill?"

"I sure did. She looked like she was going to throttle him. Teaches her though. Misty is a whore. I won't let her in here."

Grace listened to the two women as they talked, actually, gossiped more than talked. The two women were really close, and she was envious of their confidence.

"That was delicious," she said.

"Good, food is free here." Teri winked at her, and took the dishes.

The rest of the day went by without much event. Grace worked the whole day only taking a few breaks when Teri sent her off. She liked working as it helped to keep her mind occupied. The last thing she wanted to do was think about Dwayne, and how stupid she had been.

At the end of the day, the diner was still open, and she learned it would be open until around midnight. Teri left the kitchen after Daniel made his appearance. The boy was tall and muscular. She understood why he wanted to prospect for the club.

Sitting down, Teri handed her a coffee.

"You're always giving me food and drink," Grace said, smiling.

"It's a habit. I love cooking and taking care of people." Teri sat down. "Right, you've got the job."

"I have? Thank you."

Teri held her hand up. "I've got to work over a schedule. I expect you to have fun while you work here."

"Fun?"

"Yes. This may be a diner, but it's not your everyday diner. I want this to be a place for families to come and leave with a smile. I know you're a waitress, and that's supposed to be a shitty job, but I don't allow that. This is *my* diner. Dirty Fuckers give me total control over this place. I pay my waitresses good money, and I expect good service."

Grace frowned. "Did I do something wrong?"

"You were the perfect waitress. The biggest problem, I didn't see you having fun. Smile a little, Grace. Relax, no one here is going to hurt you."

Looking down into the dark brown liquid of her coffee, she sighed. "My ex, he did a number on me."

"I figured as much. You're not ready to talk about it, and I get that. Allow this job to be a place where you find yourself." Teri patted her hands. "I expect you here bright and early tomorrow. Make it seven, okay?"

"Sure."

She turned to find Suzy entering the diner.

"I'll leave you to your friend."

Teri and Suzy shared a hug, and then her friend sat in front of her. "Well, is it good news or bad?"

"It's good." She told Suzy about what Teri had instructed her.

Suzy chuckled. "Teri's amazing. You'll love her. Come on, let's get out of here."

Grace finished her coffee, licking her lips. Even the coffee at the diner was delicious. No wonder Teri wanted everything different.

The food was great, the drinks, too, and Teri wanted the atmosphere to be the same as well. She could handle that.

Fuck you, Dwayne, I'm going to move on and be happy.

MY KIND OF DIRTY

Chapter Three

Three weeks later

"So, how is the new girl coping?" Drake asked. He was at the back of the kitchen where he was helping Teri load up stuff she wanted for the annual summer fair.

"I knew it. I knew you liked her. I figured there had to be a reason for you coming by more often." Teri smiled, pointing her finger at his chest.

"I always come here."

"Ever since I employed Grace, you've been coming in twice a day, and you checked out the schedule. I saw you doing it in my office on the first week. Don't lie."

He didn't say anything, placing down the large, foil-wrapped baking dish. It was still warm, and the scents coming from it were amazing. The first week that Grace had been employed he'd watched her change. She'd gone from being this sad, reserved woman to smiling, and chatting with the customers, even the Dirty Fuckers. He wasn't stupid, and knew that Teri had told her to be more outgoing. She had a standard that she demanded from all of her employees. It was what made her different from many other diners.

"She's hot, isn't she?" Teri asked, leaning against the doorframe, and refusing him a chance to leave. "Have you noticed how long her hair is?"

Drake had a thing about long hair. Many of his fantasies involved Grace on her knees in front of him, her hair wrapped around his wrist as he pounded into her pussy, over and over again.

"What are you getting at?" he asked.

She lifted her shoulders, giving him a coy smile. "I'm just shocked you've not tried to tap that."

"From the sounds of it, you have."

"Bite me, Drake. You know I get pleasure from everything." Teri was known for loving both men and women. He'd seen many of the shows she put on for the club. Personally, he didn't want the competition in the bedroom. Threesomes were all great, but focus tended to wane a little if there was too much tit or cock. "Tell you what, I'll take this lot to the high school grounds, and you can come with Grace. She should arrive in ten minutes, and there's a second car outside. Do you think you can drive it?"

The temptation was too good to pass up, and he didn't want to miss a chance with Grace. He'd spent three weeks watching her, using every chance he got to talk to her. She wasn't the easiest person to talk to, which annoyed the fuck out of him.

"You know I can drive it."

"All right, this is going to be awesome. I hope you're ready for Grace. She's had a bad experience with some asshole. I don't know everything, but I know she doesn't trust easily."

He wondered if Suzy knew anything more about Grace. She always changed the subject when one of the customers asked her what she'd been doing with herself. She was the queen at evasion.

Grace entered the kitchen ten minutes later, wearing a pair of jeans and a shirt that was two sizes bigger than she was. "Hey," she said.

"Hey."

Fuck, hey? That's all you've got to say, asshole?

Teri came out of the kitchen wiping her hands on a towel. "Grace, you made it. I've filled one car, and I'm going to leave you and Drake to fill the second. Is that okay?"

"Wait? I can drive the second car if he wants to

go with you," Grace said. Her cheeks looked a little flushed, and it was the only sign he got that she was affected by him being near. The clothes she wore made it hard for him to read her body's response to him. He glanced down at her large tits, and he wondered if her nipples were hard for him.

"The pots are heavy, Grace. It will be easier if Drake does the heavy lifting. It's what I've had him here for, as otherwise he'd be at the high school already helping the brothers get set up."

"All you women do is use us big strapping men to lift shit for you," Drake said, finally getting a word in.

Teri tapped his chest. "You do it all so well. You'll follow me?" Teri asked.

Grace nodded. "I will. Everything you want is wrapped, right?"

"Yep. I've pointed it out to Drake."

Together they followed Teri toward the car. Grace was gripping the strap of her bag hard. She had the bag nestled between her breasts as the strap was across her body in a satchel type bag.

They both waved at Teri's disappearing car.

Alone, silence fell between them, and Drake turned to find Grace staring at him.

"I'll get the car," he said, holding the keys that Teri had given to him. Climbing behind the wheel, he reversed toward the kitchen. "Come on, Drake, you can do this. You've made it your mission to fuck the wrong kind of woman. Grace, she's totally right."

His little obsession for the young waitress had gradually built on him, surprising him. Yes, he visited the diner regularly, but he'd started to visit more since Grace began to work for Teri. That wasn't all, he found himself following her home to make sure she got there safely. He didn't let her know that he was there, simply kept a safe distance to make sure she was okay.

For three weeks he'd kept a close eye on her, and he'd not touched another woman since seeing her.

Climbing out of the car, he moved into the kitchen, hearing Grace grunting. Entering, he found her trying to lift up a lasagna pan, but it wasn't moving.

"Teri warned you it was heavy," he said.

Grace stood up abruptly, pushing some hair off her brow. "There's no way you can do that. It's back-breaking labor."

He chuckled. "You've clearly not been around the right kind of men." Drake flexed his muscles, and when he looked, he saw his Dirty Fuckers MC cut hid the evidence of his thick arms. Quickly removing his jacket, he showed her his arms. Turning to Grace, he winked at her.

One of her arms was across her stomach, and the other hand covered her mouth. The humor in her eyes wasn't hard to miss.

"I can't believe you've just flexed for me."

"Come on, touch them." He urged her, nudging his arm toward her. "Go on, feel it."

"I'm not going to feel your muscles. It's wrong."

"Don't be a wimp. Feel them."

Grace rolled her eyes and stepped toward him. She placed her thumb and finger, giving it a pinch. "Oh, hard."

It was his turn to roll his eyes. "Get a good feel of them." Grabbing her arm, he placed it over the bulging muscle. "That's a real man."

She shook her head, chuckling. "You're right. Now I guess you get to show off with the lasagna?"

"You bet your sweet ass I do."

He grabbed the lasagna tray, lifting it with ease, and carrying it toward the back of the car.

Grace whistled. "I respect your strength." She gave him a little bow. "I'm not worthy."

"You just watch this muscle man at work." He winked at her, and then kept walking in and out of the back of the kitchen. Each time he past her, he mentally berated himself. What the hell was he doing? If any of the brothers saw him now, they'd never let him live it down.

After seven trips, the car was full. Grace was closing up the kitchen and stood in the doorway. "That was fun. I'm sorry that I doubted your ability to carry."

"He-Man, that's what I am."

She chuckled, and the sound went straight to his cock. Grabbing his leather jacket, he stood with her as she locked up the kitchen. "Where's Chloe?" she asked.

"She's helping decorate the high school hall. They're using the hall, the classrooms, and the whole of the football field."

"Suzy told me that Sharon had invited several businesses to set up shop for the whole town. I've also seen lots of tourists coming through. Daniel has been running wild trying to keep up with orders. The diner has literally been heaving. I don't know if you noticed but Teri put out several tables and chairs to soak up the sun."

Talk about something else, Drake. Come on.

"How is life back in town?" he asked.

"It's great. At times it's like I never left."

He opened the car, brushing across her chest as he did. There was not a sign that she even noticed the touch. He didn't like the flash of panic in her eyes.

"We're here, that's pretty different."

The smile was back. "Yeah, an MC taking up residence had been a pretty big shock. At first I hadn't believed it."

"Surprise."

She got into the car, and he closed the door.

"Yes, it was a surprise," she said when he climbed behind the wheel. Starting up the car, he pulled away from the diner, and headed toward the high school. "I never thought for a second that a biker club would want to take up residence in Greater Falls. I'm glad you did. I love working at the diner."

"When we first came back, we had a lot of problems."

"Until the parties?" she asked.

"Parties?"

He glanced over at her to find she was once again staring at him.

"I'm not oblivious to the rumors running around about the Dirty Fuckers' parties. They're wild."

Tapping the steering wheel he focused on the road ahead of him. "What do you know of the parties?"

"I don't know anything to be honest, only what I've overheard in town. They're a pretty big deal for a lot of women. Also, Chloe is always looking happy about them. They're a big orgy or something?"

Drake sighed, looking toward her. "I can't tell you. Only women who are invited or escorted by one of the brothers are allowed to be there." Sometimes some of the club whores brought a friend. The brothers didn't mind seeing new talent.

"I'm not looking for an invitation. I'm sworn off men and partying. Right now I'm focusing on getting myself back to being me."

"What happened?" he asked. "You don't have to tell me."

"It's okay. With you, I feel I can tell you everything. Is that strange?"

Yes. "No, not at all."

"Well, when my parents were killed in a plane

crash, I didn't know what I'd do. I was eighteen at the time, so at least I didn't have to worry about finding a guardian to take me in. When I graduated school, I decided it was time for a fresh start away from all the pitying looks. It's hard to move on when everyone knows your business."

"I get that."

"I went away to college, and that was where I met Dwayne. Everything was going great. I mean, he was nice, or at least he was nice most of the time. He suggested he'd earn more with his job in accounting, so I quit school to help support him. After a short time, he started getting nasty, and then he started to get violent."

Drake wanted to kill that fucker, and he didn't even know him. Any guy who raised his hand to a woman needed taking down, and snuffing out.

"It's so embarrassing. Looking back, I was so grateful to have a boyfriend that I would blame myself for him attacking me. If my dad was still alive right now, he'd have a few choice words to say to me."

"Your father sounds like my type of guy to have a drink with."

"Yeah, he always told me to stick up for myself, and to never let anyone give me shit. I miss them, you know?"

"I don't know, darling. My parents were addicts, and put up with me. When I was old enough, I got out, and I've not looked back."

"I'm so sorry."

"No need to be sorry, but I get what you mean. They're your family. If your parents had been alive, they wouldn't have allowed this Dwayne to get a look in. He saw you were vulnerable, and he took advantage of that. You did right, getting out."

Grace smiled. "I'm kind of proud of myself

actually."

"You should be. You got away."

"Not just because of that. On that final day when I was packing, Dwayne came in while I was halfway through. He started yelling, and when he came in close with the intention of hitting me, I grabbed the bat that I had purchased, and I swung, hitting his arm. I told him to stay the fuck away from me otherwise I was going to call the cops on his nasty ass."

"Did it work?" he asked, laughing.

"He spent the rest of the day bitching but he didn't lay a finger on me, and he hasn't come after me."

This woman, she really was something, and what was worse, she didn't even see it. What the fuck was he going to do?

****

Grace loved the sound of his laughter.

"Did you kick his ass?"

"I would have done. Thinking back, I should have kicked his ass long before then." Grace hated how withdrawn she'd become with Dwayne. He'd been a total asshole, and she'd been so desperate for affection that she had made all kinds of excuses. "I was so lucky actually. Looking back, I still can't believe that I fell for his crap. I mean, what kind of man does that? I must have been so desperate for someone to love me."

"Desperate?"

"Yeah, my parents had died, and I'd not had a real boyfriend." She pointed at her body. "Look at me. It's not like any guy is going to go for me when they've got a hot, slender alternative."

"Are you fucking shitting me right now?" he asked.

"Huh?"

"You're telling me that the first guy you were

with treated you like shit because of your size?"

"Now that you put it like that?"

"No, there's no way to neatly put it. You fell for the first guy who fed you sweet words? You were a virgin?"

Grace shot him a glare. "That is a very private and personal question."

"Fucking is all part of life. We all do it, unless you're a nun, but whatever."

"How old are you?"

"Thirty-nine, babe. You?"

"Wow, you're so old. I'm twenty-five."

Drake swerved the car to a stop, and glared at her. "Thirty-nine is not old. It's experienced, and you're trying to avoid the question."

"It's none of your business."

"People fuck. It's natural."

"At the club yeah, but it's not something normal people talk about."

"Teri fucks at the club. Are you saying she's not normal?"

"You're trying to put words in my mouth, and that's not fair," Grace said, growling in frustration.

"You're a prude. That's your problem."

"I'm not a prude."

"Then tell me, were you a virgin?"

"None of your business." She folded her arms and wished he would start the car up.

"It's perfectly fine to be a prude. Your husband, when you get one, will probably stray, and when he does, you'll be sitting at home wondering where he's sticking his dick, and what he's doing while you're at home wonderi—"

"Yes! Dammit, I was a virgin, and Dwayne laughed afterward. It was the worst feeling in the world, and guess what? It hurt." She shook her head. "God, what is wrong with you men? You think you're all so damn good in bed, and it's not the case. Slam, bam, thank you, and all that. It doesn't work like that, and when he tried to have sex with me, it still hurt. The earth didn't move. There was no great explosion, it was just pain."

Silence fell on the car, and she groaned as she realized what she had told him.

"Ugh!" Releasing her seatbelt, she climbed out of the car, and started pacing back and forward. Her heart was racing, and she was so damn mad, she could spit.

She wasn't surprised when Drake got out of the car, resting against it as she paced. "Are you happy about that?" she asked.

"Do I look like I am?"

Grace paused long enough to stare at him. "No, you don't, and I'm so happy about that." She wasn't, though. This was the last thing she wanted to do. She hadn't even told Suzy about what happened. She had kept every single little detail to herself.

Bending forward, she held onto her knees as she took several deep breaths, trying to calm her rioting nerves.

Drake's scuffed boots appeared in her vision. When his hand touched her back, she couldn't help but close her eyes at the contact.

"You don't have to be afraid, baby. I've not raised my hand to a woman, and I don't intend to start now." He ran his hand up and down her back, and she took deep breaths.

"I don't want to talk about it."

"Fine, but now I'm going to talk, and you're going to listen."

Grace mumbled in agreement.

"You had a bad experience with one guy, okay? He was a total ass, and the first time for a woman is always uncomfortable, but it can turn into one of the most amazing experiences of your life with the right guy."

Grace laughed, finally easing up. She pushed some of her brown hair off her face, and stared at him. "The right guy? There's no such thing."

Drake shrugged. "Give it time."

"Have you made a woman orgasm?" she asked, and her cheeks heated. "Crap, don't answer that."

He stepped close, and she became aware that not only was she a woman, but he was a man. A large man, a biker, with thick, muscular arms that she had been touching less than thirty minutes ago. "I've had a woman screaming, and begging me to pound her pussy, Grace. Give it time, and give yourself a chance to explore and experiment."

In that moment she wondered what it would be like to have sex with Drake. *You called him old.*

"I don't think you're old."

"And I don't think you're a baby either."

They stared at each other for several seconds, and Grace didn't know if it was her, or if Drake was waiting for something to happen.

He leaned in close, and Grace didn't know what she was going to do. A car passed, honking its horn, and the moment was gone, completely gone.

Grace tensed up, stepping back a little. Shoving her hand between them, she took a deep breath. "Friends?"

Drake looked at her hand, and then at her. "Is that what you want?"

"I think it would be for the best, don't you?" Grace licked her lips. She couldn't help but wonder what it would have been like to kiss him. He was a handsome man.

He took her hand. "Friends it is." Drake squeezed her hand. "Let's get to the fair." He opened the car door for her, and she climbed back inside, feeling stupid for even leaving the damn car in the first place.

Strapping herself in, she waited for him to start the car up once again, and they were on the road.

"I think you should."

"What?" she asked.

"Experiment. Maybe get a vibrator to explore—"

"Enough, Drake. We're friends, and friends don't talk about vibrators with each other." She shook her head laughing. This she could handle. Most of her life she had always been friends with guys.

Drake was firmly in the friends pile.

MY KIND OF DIRTY

Chapter Four

The high school was swarming by the time they got there. Drake parked the car to find Teri already waiting. When he saw her smile, he shook his head, and Teri's face lost its humor. Was she trying to set them up? He didn't know.

"Showtime," he said.

Grace grabbed a pot that she could carry.

"What's going on?" Teri asked.

Drake sighed, resting his hands on his hips. "We're going to stick to being friends."

"What? Why?"

"The guy she was with was a serious asshole, and has scared her."

"So? You're a Dirty Fucker. Some guy treating her like shit shouldn't bother you."

"It doesn't."

"You're just going to give up?"

Drake glared at her. "No, but I'm not about to start bombarding her with shit she's not ready to deal with. I can handle friends."

Teri laughed. "You? You can handle being friends?"

"I can handle a lot. For instance, friends go shopping, friends have dinner, friends go to the movies, and friends hang out."

"That's a pretty big list."

"Yep, it's a pretty big list, and I intend to become Grace's new BFF."

"What's going on, guys?" Grace asked.

"Nothing. Watch my muscles at work, women." He removed his jacket, draping it over Grace's shoulder. Giving both women a view of his flexing muscles, he winked, and started to carry the pots.

James and Cora were standing with Sharon and Thomas in the main hall. There was a large table set up with food.

"Thank you so much for doing this," Sharon said.

"No problem. The men don't mind," James said.

"It's easy for you to say. You're not the one carrying all this fine food." Drake walked over to them. "What did you to?" He looked at Thomas.

"I fixed all the tables and set up the decorations."

Sharon reached out, holding Thomas's hands. "He's done wonders, don't you think? He also built the stage outside for the graduation ceremony."

"You should have been there," Thomas said.

Drake scrunched his nose up. "Nah, kids don't do it for me. Besides, it would have looked a little strange if a man who didn't have a kid suddenly turned up watching them graduate. Thinking about it freaks me the fuck out."

James laughed. "Ryan graduates next year."

"Then I will be here to see the kid, not before."

He nodded to the women, and went back to the car to help unload the food. Once that was done, he parked the car, and lost Grace in the throng of people. Tourists and locals had all come out for the good weather, and his plan to spend the time with Grace was screwed. He saw Lucy had arrived with her oldest son, Ryan, and the two youngest. Their father, Dane, was part of the Dirty Fuckers MC until he just left without a reason. Until he came back, the brothers had taken it turns to help the woman out. He gave Lucy a wave, and Ryan headed toward him.

"Hey, Drake," Ryan said.

"How's your mom?"

"She's fine. She's been a lot happier since you guys have been coming around. I even see her smile now." Ryan held onto the loops of his jeans.

"We're all one big happy family, and when Dane gets back, I'm going to kick his ass."

Ryan's smile dropped. "I hope he doesn't come back."

He paused to look at the kid. "What? I thought you wanted your dad back?"

"In the beginning I did. Mom was so hung up on him, and she was working all the time to make ends meet. Before Dad left, I didn't tell James this, but they would argue all the time."

Drake frowned. This was news to him. Whenever he saw Dane before he left, the fucker would talk constantly about being a Dad, and a husband. "They argued?"

"Yeah. She used to shout at him smelling of another woman's perfume, and of him spending his days screwing and drinking. I want Mom to move on. I want her to be happy and not think about my dad. She's not been on a date since she left."

"You're now trying to pimp your mom out?" Drake asked.

"No. Dad, he's an asshole, and I accept that now. Mom, she's beautiful, and young still. She had me when she was young. I don't want her to wait around for a guy that didn't even care to divorce her."

Drake sighed. "Do you have someone in mind?"

"There's Lewis Corn. He's a rancher just on the outskirts of town. They're friends, and he lost his wife to cancer three years ago."

"Around the time your dad left?" Drake asked.

"Is it wrong to want to arrange a date between them?" Ryan asked.

"It's not wrong, but it's not exactly right, either."

"I want her to be happy."

"Then keep getting good grades. That will work."

Several guys shouted Ryan's name, and Drake urged him to go and have fun. When he turned around, he saw that Leo and Paul were helping Lucy, taking them around the fairground.

Entering the main hall, he saw James was still with Cora talking to Sharon and Thomas. He spotted Teri removing the wrappings from the food, and there was no sign of Grace. Moving toward the woman, he grabbed a spicy potato wedge, biting into it.

"Did you see where Grace went?"

"Suzy's here, and they went off to get some cotton candy."

"I thought she was supposed to be working today?"

"What? Grace? No. It's her day off. The diner is closed. Besides, she helped me make all of this. She's one hell of a cook. Look for Pixie. He still won't take no for an answer even though she doesn't give him the time of day. Personally, I think he scares her, and I don't think Suzy's ever had sex, let alone sweaty, dirty sex." Teri shrugged.

Since settling down in Greater Falls, Teri had really grown to love the place, and she made her mark on the little town. The whole town adored her, and through her, they accepted the club. Without the club, Teri wouldn't be here, so it all worked out.

"Pixie?"

"He seems to know where Suzy is. Haven't you ever noticed he's always there when Suzy is? Besides, I'm getting tired of him buying me new underwear. With how much he's gotten me, I could open my own underwear stall, it's that bad."

Drake laughed. "He has to find a reason to buy shit?"

"If he wants to go to the shop where Suzy works."

Taking another potato wedge, he gripped Teri's shoulder. "You did good, more than good. This is all amazing."

"Thanks. I really do love it here."

"It does work for us, doesn't it?" Drake asked.

"You could settle down here, you know? Start a family. Sharon's a great principal, and I even heard the preschool and primary school rock as well."

"Are you trying to convince me? Dirty Fuckers are not going anywhere."

"It's what I like to hear," Teri said.

"We got out of all that shit years ago." The Dirty Fuckers didn't want any kind of shit that other MCs had. He'd heard of The Skulls and Chaos Bleeds, and they had more than enough crap to last them a lifetime. Dirty Fuckers were content to own their small piece of land, the club, the diner, and their other businesses. The only thing they had in common with the other two clubs was Ned Walker. They had worked for that mean motherfucker at one time. "I'm going to find some brothers."

Kissing the top of Teri's head, he left the main hall, heading out into the heat. He became aware that he didn't have his leather cut on, so all he had to do was look for the woman wearing his jacket.

Moving toward one of the first stalls, he saw Richard, the lawyer who came to the club to unleash his Dominant side, shooting at a target.

"Wow, I didn't know you did anything but work," Drake said.

"Raising money for the school, having some fun, even I have to relax at times." Richard lowered the gun, taking the stuffed bear that he'd won. If Richard wasn't a lawyer, he'd have been one of the brothers, easily. He was a tough guy.

"I thought that's why you came to the club."

"It's one of the reasons." Richard held onto the stuffed bear. "What's Chloe up to these days?"

Drake stared at the lawyer. "You're wanting to know about Chloe?"

"I've not seen around the club for a couple of weeks. Didn't know if you let her go."

"Chloe's still at the club, Richard. She also works at the diner."

"I've not seen her in the back."

Drake sighed. "Chloe's pulled away from going to the playroom. She only plays in the main room."

"Why?"

"She was worried that she was falling for you." He didn't see a reason to keep that kind of stuff secret. Chloe was a sweet woman. Her heart was in the right place, and he'd even seen her getting close with Grace and Suzy.

Club whore or not, Chloe's heart was that of an old lady. She just didn't see it, which sucked.

Drake would have taken her himself but they were friends, and he didn't want to commit to her like that.

"She didn't have to stop coming to see me," Richard said.

"Yeah, she did." He wasn't about to tell the man that Chloe had cried when she saw Richard with another woman, how he was dressed up, treating her with respect. None of the brothers would ever allow anyone to hurt one of their own, but matters of the heart were a lot harder to control.

****

"You're wearing a leather cut," Suzy said.

"I know." Grace gripped the lapels of the jacket. It was hot, but she liked the scent of Drake around her. He made her feel safe, and protected. "I like it, and he was doing a lot of carrying so I held onto it for him."

"Will he want it back?"

"Yeah, we're friends."

"I've seen Cora wearing James's jacket," Suzy said.

They were in the queue for some cotton candy, and everywhere Grace looked, there seemed to be a Dirty Fuckers leather cut. She hoped to see Drake again, but so far, no sign of him.

"Cora's an old lady. Chloe told us how things worked."

"Speaking of Chloe, I was thinking we should invite her over to our place. Have a girly night."

"What about Teri?" Grace asked.

"Her too. I like her, and her food is amazing. You should really let her taste some of the stuff you create."

"It's Teri's diner, and she has some awesome skills. I love watching her, and tasting her food."

"With you moving in with me, I'm going to have to get a bigger size. I'm ballooning, and soon I'll fill the space a size of a tank."

Grace frowned, looking at Suzy's size sixteen. The woman was gorgeous. She had large tits, and hips that were an hourglass figure. Suzy rocked the fifties style dresses, which was what she was wearing now. Her red hair was left to cascade around her body. The length looked so soft and glossy. She was a beautiful woman, who caught several men's gazes. What did Suzy see when she looked in the mirror? She behaved like she was some kind of ugly person. Grace had seen the way Pixie stared at Suzy, as did several other men.

"Don't put yourself down."

Suzy chuckled. "I'm not. I just know what I look like."

Before Grace could say anything, they were the first in the queue, and Daniel, the Dirty Fuckers prospect, was serving them up some cotton candy.

"I didn't know you were going to be here today," Grace said.

"I help out where I can. It's the role of a Prospect within the club." Daniel handed them both some candy and a soda.

"I'll take care of this," Pixie said, handing over some cash.

Suzy tensed up. "That's okay, we can affor—"

"Don't you worry about it, babe. It's the least I can do. Cheeseburger," Pixie said.

Grace stood while Suzy looked like she wanted to say otherwise.

"Thank you," Grace said, moving away from the queue. No one in the long line mentioned the fact Pixie had moved in. "He's got a thing for you." She made sure to speak in a whisper so no one could hear.

"I don't know. I think he just can't handle the fact I said no."

"Well, ladies, what are you doing today?" Pixie asked, coming to stand with them.

"What are you doing?" Suzy asked.

"Spending some time with you. Do you have a problem with that?"

Grace glanced around at all of the women staring at Pixie as if they wanted to strip him naked, and have his babies. This wasn't uncomfortable at all. *Not.*

Suzy frowned. "Sure, fine."

Staring at Pixie, he saw that he looked perplexed at the lack of excitement from Suzy.

Feeling like a third wheel, Grace stared around

the large football field wondering what the hell to do.

"I've got to go to the bathroom. Will you hold these for me?" Suzy asked. She was gone a second later, and Grace held her soda and candy.

Pixie sighed. "She's really a tough cookie, isn't she?"

Grace tilted her head to the side, watching the large biker. "Do you even like her?"

"Yeah, I wouldn't be here if I didn't."

"How do you know if you like her?" Grace asked.

"What?"

"I've not seen you trying to get to know her."

"I've tried asking her out."

"She's said no, and you just leave."

"This is the hardest I've ever worked for any pussy," Pixie said.

Grace scrunched up her nose. "You're not going to get to Suzy with that attitude. If you just want to fuck her, walk away. She deserves better than you."

She moved away, leaving Pixie to his own, single minded attitude. Waiting outside of the toilet, she smiled at customers who came into the diner.

"Is he gone?" Suzy asked.

"Yeah. Don't worry about him. He's an asshole."

Suzy cringed. "He's persistent, but he just wants to fuck. I don't like him."

She told Suzy what he said to her, and they both looked disgusted. "See, why would I want to be with him? He's gross."

"I told him he didn't deserve you."

They walked around the large playing field, eating, and talking.

"I'm thinking we should get a dog."

"A dog? We're working all the time," Grace said.

"I know, but I've always wanted a dog, and at the

trailer it was impossible to have a pet."

Grace didn't want her friend to go without, so she tried to think about it. "We could take turns walking it."

"It will be fun. What kind of dog?"

"Labrador?" Grace suggested. She loved dogs but hadn't owned one herself either.

"It's too big. Our apartment is nice, but not that nice. A Labrador needs a lot of space. What about a beagle?"

"Nope, they require a lot of exercise, more than we have time for."

"Fine, Pomeranian it is."

"Aw," Grace said. "They're going to be so cute and fluffy."

"You think so?"

"Yeah. We'll have to be careful though so we don't mistake it for a cushion. Do you want to pick one up next week?"

"I'll look online, and see if there are any breeders," Suzy said.

They rounded a corner, and there was Drake with another man carrying a bear.

"Grace, I've been looking for you," Drake said.

"I've been here." She turned to the man with the bear, giving him a smile.

"Richard, this is Grace. Grace, this is Richard."

"It's nice to meet you." Her hands were full.

"This is Suzy," she said, looking toward her friend.

Once the introductions were done, Suzy left the group as she found someone to talk to, leaving Grace alone with Richard and Drake.

"Nice bear," Grace said.

"Hey, guys," Chloe said, walking up to them.

Richard turned toward the other woman, and he

seemed to tense up. Turning toward Chloe, Grace was surprised to see her in a conservative pale pink dress. "Have you seen Suzy?"

"I just passed her. She had seen someone she wanted to talk to." Chloe joined them, and her smile dropped when she saw Richard. "Hi, I didn't see you there. I didn't think you'd come here," she said.

"I live in Greater Falls, and I used to go to this high school."

The once bubbly woman looked totally uncomfortable.

"Can I talk with you?" Richard asked.

"Erm, sure, I guess."

Grace moved beside Drake, watching them.

"There's tension between them, right? That's not just me?"

"There's a shitload of tension between the two."

"I like Chloe. He better not be hurting her."

"The club will hurt him if he even tries. Chloe, she's a darling, sweet, and caring. Don't worry, we've got her back, and we'll take care of her."

Grace nodded, taking a bite of her cotton candy.

"So, I was wondering if you'd like to go and see a movie with me?" he asked.

Glancing up at him, she bit her lip. "Like a date?"

"No, not like a date. Like two friends going out, watching a movie, of your choice, of course, and maybe getting some dinner afterward."

She was a little disappointed. *Why are you disappointed? This is what you wanted, duh!*

"I'd like that."

"How about Monday night?"

Grace shook her head. "I'm working the evening shift. I don't get off 'til midnight. I'm good next Friday if you can wait. We don't even know what's showing."

"Something good should be showing. I'll pick you up around seven?" Drake said.

"Sounds good to me." She offered up some candy. "Seeing as you're my friend, and you can't take your gaze away from my candy, have some." He took a bite while staring into her eyes. "Tastes good."

"Hell yeah."

Offering him a drink of soda, she walked beside him as they continued to enjoy the fun.

****

"You look different," Richard said.

Chloe glanced down at the pale pink summer dress and felt her cheeks heat. Richard had only ever seen her in club clothes, the short skirts, and fuck me jeans. The dresses were part of her more normal life when she didn't want to draw attention to herself. "We're not in the club." Pausing near the bleachers, she turned to him. "What did you want to talk to me about?"

She saw the bear he was holding but averted her gaze. This man had the power to unravel her in ways she didn't even understand or like. The feelings he inspired inside her were part of the reason she had stopped going to the playrooms of the clubhouse. She still played with the club men as she did love having strong arms wrapped round her when she was sleeping. None of them was the right man. She wasn't a fool. There was no way Richard would go with a woman like her. Outside of the playroom, he never gave her the time of day.

"I wanted to see how you were."

"I'm good. Cute teddy bear," she said, trying to change the subject.

He held it out. "I won it for you."

"Oh." She took the bear, smiling down at it. "Thank you."

"I don't want this to be hard for us." He went to

touch her, and Chloe pulled away.

"There's no need for this to be a problem between us, Richard. We're completely different people."

"Chloe?"

"What?" *Don't cry. Don't cry.*

She forced herself to stare at the man who had worked his way into her heart. The same man she had watched take another woman out to dinner. She had been with him so many times, and yet not once had he wanted anything to do with her after a scene they'd shared together. She meant nothing to him, and that was what she needed to remember.

"I don't want you to stop coming to the playrooms."

Chloe's heart broke. That was all she was good for. The playrooms. All of her life she'd been told she was only ever good for one thing. Men wouldn't want anything to do with her unless she spread her legs.

Glancing down at the bear, Chloe came to a decision. It was time for her to take a step back from the club. If she didn't, she would lose herself. She'd go and see Teri about giving her more hours at the diner.

"I can't take this," she said, handing him back the bear.

He didn't take it. "I won it for you."

"Give it to that woman you took to the Italian restaurant." She had been at the local grocery store across the street. Chloe hadn't gone hunting him. She wasn't that kind of woman. "I won't be coming to the playrooms anymore. Goodbye, Richard." Turning on her heel, she made a way toward James. It was time for her to cut loose from the club.

Chapter Five

"You don't have to leave," James said. Drake stood just inside the room, watching as Chloe packed up her stuff. Suzy was waiting outside with Grace. The two women had offered Chloe a bed to sleep in. They'd been near Cora and James when Chloe dropped the bombshell. Of course, she'd been crying while she said something.

Drake had seen Richard staring after her even though he'd not done anything to stop the woman.

"It's time I moved on, James. I told you I wasn't going to be at the club much longer."

"How are you going to support yourself?" Cora asked.

"I've spoken to Teri, and she can give me extra hours at the diner. Daniel has other jobs to do, so I'll be taking over from him."

She filled a large duffel bag with clothes. He noticed she only owned two pairs of shoes and a pair of pumps she already had on. Staring at her now, he had to wonder how she ever survived at the club. She looked out of place. Even the club women that went to the high school to have some fun had dressed in far more revealing clothing, short, tight skirts. Chloe looked like she had stepped out of a real estate advertisement.

Once she had everything, she came toward them. "It's time for me to move on."

"Is it Richard? I can stop him coming to the club," James said.

"It's not him. It's me. It's time I moved on, and I'm going to do that." Chloe turned to Cora. "May I hug him?"

"Sure. I know you don't mean anything by it other than being friendly," Cora said.

Chloe wrapped her arms around James. It had to

be the friendliest hug he'd ever seen from the young woman.

"Thank you so much for everything you've done for me. You gave me a home, and you didn't leave me rotting in that club. For that, I'll always be in your debt. It's time for me to find myself now." She turned around to look at them, and several of the brothers looked truly heartbroken. Several of the club pussy looked more than happy to see her go. Drake wasn't going to be fucking her ever again. He wanted Grace, and he saw both women were becoming friends. "I'm not going to be a stranger to you guys. I'll be working at the diner, and if it's okay with James, I'll come to a few parties every now and then. It's not goodbye at all. I'm not leaving town."

On the way out of the club, Chloe hugged everyone. Not one guy let her go without throwing his arms around her.

On the way out, Grace was waiting beside the car with the trunk popped open. Chloe placed her bag in the trunk, and he stood close to them.

"Are you sure about this?" Grace asked.

"It's time I moved on. I'm only going to get my heart broken here. That is all my fault, just so you know. No one else is to blame for this."

Drake frowned at that. No one here was going to break Chloe's heart. She never let anyone close enough.

Richard, she did.

He was going to kill that bastard. Richard was the one to make her cry as well. He'd bet every single cent he owned that he was the cause of this reaction. The club was going to want to have a word with Richard. There was no way he was getting away with this kind of shit. He knew that Chloe had tried to take a step back because of her feelings for Richard, but this was different.

Richard had gone looking for her. He knew this because Richard had asked about Chloe. Yes, Chloe was a club girl, but she was one of the good ones.

Chloe climbed into the passenger seat, and Grace hesitated. "We'll take care of her."

"I thought it was just a two bedroom apartment."

"We can share. The beds are pretty big. We'll figure something out. We're all women here." She ran fingers through her hair. "Do you still want to go and see a movie?"

"Yes." He gripped her waist, and leaned in close, kissing her cheek. "Take care. Call me when you get back to your apartment."

"I don't have your number."

"Chloe does. Get it from her, and I'll be waiting."

Grace nodded. "Bye."

Stepping away from the car, Drake sighed.

"Is anyone going to tell me what the fuck is going on?" Jerry asked.

Several of the brothers nodded their head in agreement.

"She was perfectly fine this morning," Pixie said.

"Something clearly upset her," Caleb said. He had his arm wrapped around Kitty Cat, who was close to them like Chloe was.

"Richard," Drake said. "The last time I spoke to her she was talking to him. It makes perfect sense. She's been pining after him for some time."

"I saw him give her a bear," Cora said. "He wouldn't hurt her."

"This is not the kind of hurt that comes from being called names," James said. "I think it's time we pay our lawyer a visit. I'm not happy about this, and I want to know what the hell has been going on."

Several of the brothers volunteered. In the end,

MY KIND OF DIRTY

James took him, Caleb, Pixie, and Damon along for the ride, leaving the others to assist Teri in cleaning up. Cora went home to deal with whatever she had to deal with.

They each straddled their bikes, and took off toward the office where Richard had set up shop. He was a well respected lawyer who helped the Dirty Fuckers out of a few pickles along the way. Regardless of how many problems Richard had helped, it didn't mean they would allow him to walk over one of their own, club whore or not. They didn't like the fact Chloe had left the club. She wanted an entire separation from the club.

They entered Richard's office and ignored the young secretary on the front desk. They didn't even knock, simply walked into the office. Drake was ready to beat the shit out of the fucker.

Richard was on the phone, and the moment he saw them, he hung up. "What can I do for you?"

"You can tell us what you did to Chloe?" James asked, resting his knuckles on the desk, and glaring at the other man.

The calm, relaxed lawyer disappeared. "Not that I think it's any of your business. What's wrong with her?"

"She decided to leave the club. She's moved in with Grace and Suzy. Are you going to tell me why? You're the only problem I see. Did you treat her wrong when you took her to the private rooms?"

Richard cursed, standing up. "I'd never do anything to hurt her. I tried talking to her. I even tried to give her the fucking bear—"

"Chloe's not the kind of woman you try to bribe," Pixie said, growling each word out.

"It wasn't a bribe. I won the fucking bear, and I gave it to Chloe. She didn't take it anyway, and she walked the fuck away from me. I figured she was going back to the club." Richard ran fingers through his hair.

"She was crying when she came to us, but she wouldn't tell us why."

"Fuck. This is, I don't know. I miss her, okay? She's not in the playrooms, and I fucking miss her." Richard stopped, dropping his hands. "She told me to give the bear to someone else."

"She saw you with someone else. Chloe is not like every other woman you've ever met," Damon said. "She hurts easily, and she loves with her whole heart. Most of her life she hasn't known what protection really is. There are nights she would do whatever any guy wanted just so long as at the end of it, you wrapped your arms around her, and didn't let go until the sun came up."

That was even news to Drake, but he'd never had a problem with holding Chloe close. Considering she made him happy on the nights he'd taken her, he figured holding her was the right thing to do.

"I asked if she was going to go back to the playroom, and she just changed. She handed me back the bear, and told me it wouldn't be a good thing. I'd never hurt Chloe."

"She's in love with you," James said. "It's why she's trying to create some distance."

"Fuck, I had no idea."

"If I hear you hurt her we'll be doing a hell of a lot more than talking. Chloe may not be part of the club anymore, but she asked for our protection, and we've given it to her. Don't go near her again, unless she wants you to."

****

"Are you sure about this?" Grace asked, looking into the back of the car.

"Yeah, I'm more than sure. What about you two? I know it's only a two bedroom apartment."

"I have a king size bed, so you can sleep on that,

if you want? Or there's the couch," Suzy said. "There's not going to be any space for you to have sex if that's what you're after."

"If I need sex I can always revisit the club. It's easy that way."

"My bed is also available. It's not a sex thing either, more a friends thing."

"We can go and buy a sofa bed. You know, one of those sofas that when you pull it out, it turns into a bed," Suzy said.

"So, we're buying a puppy and a sofa bed," Grace asked.

"Oh, we're getting a puppy?" Chloe asked, leaning forward. "I love dogs and cats as well."

"The apartment's not that big, but it will do for a Pomeranian. Tonight while Grace is cooking, we'll go online and see if there's any for sale from a breeder."

Chloe squealed, clapping her hands.

"So, are you going to tell us why you're leaving a bunch of hot men?" Suzy asked. "It's really weird. You're part of the club, right?"

Chloe sighed.

"If you think they're so hot, why don't you date Pixie?" Grace asked.

"Yeah, honey, why not?" Chloe asked.

"Tell her what he said to you on the football field today. There's no way I'm dating him, not ever. He's a pig."

Grace told Chloe what Pixie had said about Suzy. Even Chloe wrinkled her nose. "Pixie's not the sweetest guy in the bunch. If you ask me I think it's because he's always trying to do better than James."

"They're brothers, right?" Suzy asked.

"Yep, and something went down with Cora, and Pixie has been trying to prove himself ever since. I don't know, maybe he's trying to prove that he has a bigger dick or something." Chloe shrugged. "He's still a good fuck though."

Suzy swerved the car. "You've slept with him?"

"I've fucked him. There's a difference. He's good in bed, great, and if you're looking for a good long night, Pixie is your man."

Grace glanced over at Suzy and saw her face heating. "What's up?"

"Nothing."

"You do know what sex feels like, right?" Chloe asked.

Suzy shook her head. "No."

"You've not had sex?" Grace asked. Even though she had a limited experience with her evil ex, Dwayne, she still wasn't a virgin.

"No, I'm a virgin." Suzy got the car under control, and kept on driving.

"Wow, I don't think Pixie knows that," Chloe said.

"It's not something I go out and advertise."

"How have you never had sex?" Grace asked. She really didn't understand why.

"It's easy. I wasn't asked out a whole lot, and when I was, if I didn't like the guy, I didn't go. If I did go, I didn't put out on the first opportunity." Suzy shrugged, pulling into the parking lot of the apartment building, Grace climbed out, grabbing Chloe's bag from the trunk. She handed the other one to Chloe, and they followed Suzy into the building. Of course they lived on the top floor, and that weekend the elevator had work being done to fix the squeaking.

They climbed the stairs, and by the time they made it to their apartment, they were all out of breath.

"Okay, I thought I was fit," Chloe said. "I spend a

great deal of time on my feet, but that took the puff right out of me."

Both women agreed with her.

Entering, Grace kicked the door closed, and collapsed on the nearest sofa. "Home sweet home."

"Or apartment sweet apartment," Suzy said. "It's not a lot, but it's home, and it beats living in a trailer with your parents."

"Do you still see your parents?" Grace asked.

"No." Suzy shuddered. "They spent most of my life telling me how I'd ruined theirs. I'm waiting to see if they will change their lives now that I'm gone. It has been five years, and guess what? They're still drinking and partying at the trailer. I see them at the grocery store with a trolley filled with booze. I ignore them, and they ignore me, which I'm more than happy about."

"I don't have a family," Chloe said.

"You don't?"

"When I was born, I was left on the doorstep of a church. The priest who was there took me to an orphanage, and then I was passed around for foster homes. I suffer with asthma you see, and none of the parents wanted the cost of keeping a sick kid. Back then, I was really sick."

"I didn't know you had asthma," Grace said.

"It's one of the reasons I don't stay in the main part of the club all the time. The smoke turns me into a coughing, red, puffy mess. It's easier to go to the playrooms where smoke isn't a problem. Richard, he never smoked. He always said that the smell was disgusting."

Grace saw the pain that flashed in Chloe's eyes. "You love him?"

"Yeah, and that's the problem. He'd never pick me if given the choice."

"You don't know that," Suzy said. They all sat on the large sofa, each resting their head on each other's shoulder.

"I do. I saw him one day. He took someone else out on a date at a fancy restaurant. He doesn't even talk to me after he gets what he wants." Chloe's lip protruded. "Life sucks sometimes."

"It really does."

"We're quite a team," Grace said.

"The virgin, the whore, and the saint."

"I'm not a saint," Grace said.

"Okay, the slave?"

Grace laughed. "I'm no one's slave."

"Go cook, wench," Suzy said, pointing at the kitchen.

They all burst into a fit of giggles.

"Drake asked me to go to the movies with him."

"Really?" Chloe asked. "What did you say?"

"We're going as friends so I didn't see a problem."

"You don't want to date him?" Suzy asked.

"I'm not ready to date."

"Drake's a nice guy." Chloe tapped her leg. "He'd be good to you, and he's nice."

"Nice is always good, much better than being vulgar. What does Pixie expect me to do? Fall for him because he says he wants to fuck me?"

"Men are weird."

"Completely weird, and boring," Suzy said.

"Don't forget they can be assholes as well."

They all sighed and snuggled up against each other.

"This is nice," Chloe said.

"What should I wear to the movies?" Grace asked. "It's not a date. It's an event between friends. Am

I allowed to dress like a slob?"

"Slob? He's still a guy."

"But he has put himself in the 'friends' category. Doesn't that mean the rules don't apply?" Grace turned to look at her two friends.

"I'd go with jeans and a shirt, or maybe a sweet looking dress, like this one. Something cute that says you're a woman, but friendly enough so he knows you're not going to put out," Chloe said.

"We'll be here to dress you," Suzy said. "You're going to be in good hands."

Chapter Six

Drake sat in the middle of Grace's apartment. Chloe and Suzy were standing in front of him. It had already been a week since Chloe had left the clubhouse, and she had yet to make an appearance. The brothers were missing her, and he missed her company.

"So, how have you been?" Drake asked.

Grace had run behind at the diner as there had been a mad rush with a large group of tourists coming to Greater Falls.

"Great, how are you?" Chloe asked.

"Good."

"What are your intentions to our girl?" Suzy asked, folding her arms across her breasts. Staring at the woman in her pajamas, which hugged every single curve, he saw what Pixie wanted so damn bad.

The brother was moping about Suzy as she had turned him down once again.

"When are you going to put Pixie out of his misery?"

"Never. He's got a club full of women to serve that pesky need of his. Answer my question."

Running fingers through his hair, he blew out a breath. "We're going to watch a movie, and I'll take her to dinner or something. I've got no intention of hurting her, or fucking her."

"Are you going to take her to the club?" Chloe asked.

He stared at her. "She's not ready to see the club."

"Suzy, would you come and help me?" Grace said, shouting for them to hear.

"Excuse me." Suzy walked across the living space toward one of the doors on the far right.

"Why would you ask about the club?"

"She's not going to be ready to see that place, and especially not the backrooms either."

"When are *you* going to stop by the club?"

"I'm not. I'm taking a break, and I see the guys when they come to eat at the diner."

"You're cutting us out of your life?" Drake asked.

"No, not at all." Chloe unfolded her arms and dropped down beside him. "I need to do this."

"I get it, believe it or not, I do." He patted her knee, offering her comfort. "The guys miss you."

"They miss having a willing woman to suck their cock."

"I don't think it's about that. They miss you being with them, holding you."

Chloe sighed. "I always worried that I was too needy."

"You'd be surprised how many guys are just as needy." He rested his head on hers.

"Don't hurt Grace."

"I'm not going to."

"I think she'd like it at the clubhouse, as weird as that sounds. She's not had a lot of experience."

"That's a long way off. She wants to be friends."

"Her ex really did a number on her, and now she has a hard time trusting anyone. It sucks, it really does, but there's not a lot we can do." Chloe pulled away. "Take care of her though."

"Always."

He turned as the door opened, and Grace walked out.

"I'm really sorry about that. I didn't mean to take my time." Her hair fell around her in curls, and she wore an ankle length blue dress with slender straps. She looked utterly beautiful.

He had some blue jeans and a black shirt underneath his Dirty Fuckers MC leather cut.

"I don't mind waiting. Teri better be paying you overtime."

"She is. It was a mad rush. Are you ready to go?"

"Yep." He turned to the other women. "We'll be late so don't wait up."

Pressing his hand on her back, he moved them out of the apartment. They walked to the end of the long corridor, and stepped on the elevator.

"This wasn't working when Chloe moved in with us. We had to walk up carrying her case. We all collapsed on the sofa completely out of breath."

He chuckled. "You're nervous."

"A little bit. I've only ever gone to the movies with the girls. This is all new."

Drake took hold of her hand. "Don't stress about it. You're safe with me."

"I know. I feel comfortable with you." She squeezed his hand, and he didn't let go of her.

They made it out toward the car.

"Crap, I'm so pleased you got a car. I didn't even think about it."

"Don't worry. I wasn't going to make you ride on the back of my biker for our first date. I'm not that careless. One day soon I'll take you for a ride." He opened the door, and helped her inside. *God, Drake, you're sounding like a pussy.*

This was not the kind of man he was. He took what he wanted, and women begged him to fuck them. Grace had yet to even give him a sign that she wanted more.

Once behind the wheel, he pulled out of the parking lot, and headed in the direction of the movies.

"So, what do you do?" she asked.

"What do you mean?"

"I'm a waitress. What do you do?"

"I work for the club. The main clubhouse opens up to certain clients who want to have fun. I help out at the diner, and we're also expanding our businesses. We're thinking of opening up a bar, seeing as Randy closed his a couple of months ago. Richard is looking at acquiring some land with the right to build. We're going into property."

"So you do a bit of everything."

"The brothers get paid an income for their service to the club. I'm more than happy with the arrangement. I'd never be the kind of man who can do a nine-to-five job. Caleb, he deals with the numbers, and is the most desk-bound of us all. It's what drew us to the life on the road."

"Has it taken some adapting to live in Greater Falls?" she asked.

"In the beginning there was some pessimism about moving, and settling down in one place."

"What changed your mind?"

"I'm getting older, and I wasn't going to be able to ride my bike for eternity or until I die. I'm a realist. I also want a family, and the only way for that to happen is by settling down in one place."

"You're happy?"

"Very much so. If I didn't settle down, I wouldn't be able to take you on a date."

"That's a good line. We're not on a date, remember? We're two friends having fun."

If you believe that, baby, I'll let you keep believing it.

It took no time at all before he was pulling into the movie parking lot. There was a short queue, and they joined the back.

"Do you know what you want to watch?" she asked.

"Not a clue."

"Did you even think check to see what was playing?"

"Nope. I figured it would be a nice surprise for us both."

"Are you going to want to watch car chasing and death?" she asked.

He laughed. "Stereotyping or what? Will you be 'hearts and flowers, and I'll love you to the day I die'?"

Grace wrinkled her nose. "Please, I know that love like that is reserved for movies and books. It's not real."

"Wow, talk about bad mood."

"Men cheat, women cheat, and love doesn't really play a big part. We need it to pretend, but it's not real."

Drake shook his head. "I have to disagree. I've seen James and Cora together. They're in love, and it's much better than books and movies. Sharon and Thomas."

"Ha, you see I heard a rumor they almost divorced because someone was interfering in their lives. Misty, the whore who likes to fuck married men. She's also fucking Bill that gym teacher who came into the diner with Stacey. It's sad really."

"Okay, so no romance, no guns and death. What about horror, or are you a chicken?"

"Horror works for me. It's a lot easier to watch." She hummed as they got closer to the main desk. There was a paranormal horror playing, which wasn't his ideal for being a date movie. He'd improvise.

They got their tickets, popcorn, sodas, and made their way into the main theater. Grace also failed to help as she took the center seats in the center of the room.

There was not going to be any chance of making out.

Maybe the movie would be terrifying enough that she'd pounce on him. He could hope.

Sitting down, he held onto the soda, and Grace held the popcorn.

"It's pretty busy."

"It's a Friday night, and the theater has air conditioning."

What the fuck are you doing? Talking about air conditioning.

Fuck.

He was never going to get Grace to take him seriously, and he wanted her to.

Running a hand down his face, he stretched out, and did the old style move of putting his arm around her shoulders. She didn't push him away or start to scream at him. Keeping his hand there, he started to relax as the movie started up. So far so good.

Trailers started playing, and Grace leaned in close telling him which movies she'd like to see. He made a mental note so that he could take her out again.

Once the movie started up, he rested the soda between his thighs, and leaned across to take some popcorn. He teased her hair, stroking the length. Every now and then, Grace would jump, and he'd be there, holding her.

His cock pressed against the zipper of his jeans. Grace was against his side, and he got a good sight of her tits pushed together. He wanted to taste those tits, to watch them bounce as he fucked into her tight pussy.

It had been four weeks since he'd been with a woman. Four weeks since a nice tight pussy wrapped around his cock, squeezing him tightly.

Soon.
Soon.

He hoped that with the chanting, he'd be able to start believing his own words. Glancing down at Grace, he saw she was oblivious to his need.

It was going to be a torturous time, but he'd handle it.

He didn't have much choice.

****

Grace dumped the empty container in the trash, following behind Drake. He took hold of her hand, and she squeezed his hand tightly. The movie had been good, scary, and safe. She never usually went for scary movies unless she had a large pillow she could look around, and if Suzy was there. Never had she imagined going to the cinema to see a scary movie.

Horror seemed easier and safe.

It was the safest choice.

Sitting next to Drake while romantic, possibly erotic, scenes played out would be too damn hard. Her relationship with Dwayne hadn't been earth shattering, but she had a feeling the earth would indeed move with him. Grace had listened to Chloe as she talked about time at the clubhouse. Chloe either spent time in her bed, or in Suzy's, or all three of them would stay in the same bed, watching movies.

They cleared the busy theater and walked into the warm night air.

"Fuck me," Drake said, removing his leather jacket. He took her hand once again, and they walked toward the car. "Are you hungry?"

Her stomach growled, and she chuckled. "Starved."

"Diner?"

"It's the only place in town that has decent food, and I'm more than happy to see Teri again." She liked her boss.

MY KIND OF DIRTY

Drake opened the car, and she climbed inside.

"You surprised me," he said.

"Why?"

"Horror? You didn't strike me as a horror girl, more of a romance girl. I didn't mind watching a romance."

Grace sighed. "I'm not going to lie. I usually love watching romance. Horror I watch at home with plenty of times to pause the film so that I can enjoy it, and not be afraid."

"Why didn't you want to watch a romance?"

"Wouldn't it be uncomfortable?"

"No."

"Really? It wouldn't have made you uncomfortable seeing people making love on the screen?"

Drake laughed. "Babe, I've seen worse than a couple pretending to get it on."

"You watch porn?"

He sighed. "What I'm about to tell you can't go anywhere else. You can't tell your friend, Suzy."

"Why not?"

"Pixie doesn't want Suzy to know."

"Ugh, maybe you shouldn't tell me. I'm with Suzy on this one. He's a pig."

"He's got a way about him."

"It's not charming, far from it."

"Look, it'll be private. Between you and me. When Pixie is ready, he'd take Suzy, and she'd know the truth."

Grace nibbled her lip, wondering what she should do. She didn't want to keep anything from her friend, but she also didn't want to be in the dark.

"Fine. I won't tell Suzy, but it better not be one of those things that if you tell me, you're going to have to kill me."

"I won't kill you, baby."

"So, if you don't watch porn, what do you watch?"

Did she really want to know what he watched?

"At the club, when you get inside, you'll discover that it's very open, very free. We don't have any rules. Obviously men and women are there because they want to be. It's consensual."

"What you're telling me isn't scary."

"We don't have sex in our bedrooms, Grace. We fuck where we want to fuck. There's a main room, and if you see a man fucking a woman, or a woman taking several cocks at the same time, that's natural. There's also a playroom at the back of the club. That's for more personal and private use."

Grace was shocked. She knew sex clubs and stuff like that were all popular right now. There had been enough media coverage of it on the news. She'd never actually been to one. Dwayne didn't even like having sex with the light on, not that she'd enjoyed their sex life. It had been boring. She'd lain on her back, while he climbed on, rutted, moaned, and came. Her sex life in a few choice words, and even now, she was ashamed of it.

"So by porn, you watch the real life stuff. You don't need to go paying per view or something like that."

He pulled into the diner's parking lot.

"No, I don't."

"Wow, I really didn't need to worry about watching a romance. Next time, that's what we're watching." She tried to make light of it, but all she felt was stupid. She had made a big deal about them being friends, and it hadn't mattered, not really. He had more than enough sex and women at the club. She'd seen many of the club whores at the diner.

Crap. Tears filled her eyes, and she forced herself to look out of the window. "We're here," she said. Climbing out of the car, she entered the diner. "I'm just going to use the bathroom."

She didn't look behind her, and made her way straight toward the toilet. Entering the stall, she sat down on the toilet, and took deep breaths.

You want to be friends, and of course he's more than fine with that. He's got what he wants at the clubhouse.

"Grace, are you okay?" She heard Teri call out her name, and she felt even more stupid.

"I'm fine. I'll be out in a moment."

"Drake told me what he said to you. He's worried about you."

"No need to be worried. I'm more than fine." She wiped the tears underneath her eyes, and did her best to suck up the pain of what his words had caused.

Flushing the toilet to keep on with the pretense that she had indeed needed the toilet, she left the cubicle, and Teri was there, arms folded.

"He wants to be with you, Grace."

"You don't have to stick up for him or anything. I get it, I really do."

"I don't think you do. You look like you've gotten the wrong end of the stick, and I find that sad to witness."

Grace sighed. She seemed to be doing that a lot just lately, and it was annoying the hell out of her. The last thing she wanted to do was keep on sighing, and making out she was upset. She was stronger than this, and she was determined to prove it.

"Drake and I are friends. I shouldn't have been so concerned about him thinking there would be more. He's got the club, and I'm fine with that."

Teri gave her a sad smile. "You're lying to yourself. Drake's not been with a woman since he first saw you."

Grace shook her head. "I doubt that."

"One day you'll see the truth. You're okay."

Staring at her reflection, Grace was more than happy that she hadn't made a mess of herself. There was no evidence of crying.

Success.

"I'm fine."

"Let's go on out."

Leaving the bathroom, she saw that Drake had taken a booth near the front of the diner. She took a seat opposite him and picked up the menu even though she knew it better than he probably did. "I can recommend a lot—"

"I haven't fucked a woman at the club, Grace, and I don't intend to. I don't want you to be nervous about this."

"I'm not nervous. Whatever you want to do with your life that's up to you." She gave him a smile. "We're still going to be friends, and that is not going to be a problem." She reached out, patting his hand. "Now, let's eat."

Daniel, the Prospect, took their order, and then left them alone.

They started talking about the movie when several of the club members entered the diner. Pixie, Caleb, James, Cora, Kitty Cat, and Jerry entered the diner.

All of the Dirty Fuckers gathered around their table. She noticed that Drake looked a little annoyed about that. She also spotted a woman near Pixie, and he pulled her down into his lap, touching the inside of her thigh.

There was no way Grace was ever going to convince her friend to date that man. He was vulgar.

"How was the movie?" Cora asked.

"It was good."

Grace offered up her fries as Cora stared at her plate hungrily.

"Thank you, I'm starving."

Sipping her coffee, Grace felt completely out of place.

"Did you see how much dick she took? She swallowed to my balls," Jerry said.

Heat filled Grace's face.

"She loves dick almost as much as this bitch here does, don't you?" Pixie asked, cupping the woman's cheek.

Glancing across the table, she smiled at Drake. "Would you mind taking me home?"

"Sure."

"You don't have to leave," James said.

"It's fine. I've got to take Grace home."

"You can stop by the club," Kitty Cat said.

"No." Grace snapped the word out. "I'm tired."

She moved around the table, staying as far away from Pixie as she could. She really didn't like him.

Once again, she was back in the car, and they were driving toward the apartment.

"I want to see you again."

"Don't you think it's a waste of time?" she asked. "I'm not like your other friends."

"Exactly. Didn't you like spending time with me today?"

"I can't give you what you want."

"All I want right now is to have some fun, take you out, and for us to get to know one another. I've not asked you to come to the club or to fuck you. I'm giving you your space."

"If you're sure?"

"I'm more than sure. I want this friendship. Did you have fun tonight?"

"I did."

"Then let's keep on having some fun."

Grace nodded. "I'm not going to help Pixie."

He chuckled. "He's got a long way to go before Suzy will look at him. One day he'll change."

"I doubt that."

"You'll be surprised. I never thought I'd see James settle down, yet he's not looked at another woman since Cora."

He pulled up outside of her apartment.

She climbed out and was surprised when he did the same.

"You don't have to come up."

"I'm going to make sure you get to your apartment safely."

Together they entered the building, going to the elevator. Grace stared at their reflections in the elevator doors. He was so tall and strong. He'd not put on his leather cut, and without it she saw his bulging muscles. She licked her lips and forced herself to look away.

Once outside of her apartment, she opened the door. "I had fun tonight."

"Good."

Against all of her best intentions, she grabbed his arm, and pressed a kiss against his cheek. "Thank you."

MY KIND OF DIRTY

Chapter Seven

One week later

"What are we doing?" Grace asked, climbing out of the large truck.

"We're going to get some more furniture for the club."

They were outside of the mall, and after last night's fight between Leo and Pixie, they had trashed the clubhouse's tables and chairs. Leo and Pixie were redecorating the main room, and he'd drawn the short straw for picking out furniture. He'd called ahead to Grace as he knew it was her day off. Chloe was working this Friday, so Grace was free to come with him.

She was also hunting for stuff to take a new puppy. Suzy had found a breeder with a Pomeranian. They were going to pick the little guy up next week, and he'd volunteered to take them all.

For the past week since their good and bad date, he'd been stopping by the diner more regularly, bugging her. He talked to her about everything. He played her music, and discovered what she liked. She loved everything from country to rock to indie. They shared their all-time favorite movies, and he'd even started reading a selection of her books. In turn, he'd gone online, purchased her an e-reader, and filled it up with erotic romance books. He wanted to get her hot and horny, and he also wanted her thinking about him as she did.

At night he lay in his bed, wondering if she was reading a book, thinking about him, and touching herself. It drove him crazy.

He and his hand had become reacquainted in the last couple of days. His brothers thought he was being a pussy by not simply taking her. Grace had been with a guy who took what he wanted. This time, he wanted Grace to be ready, and not vulnerable.

"You've been moved in a long time, and you're only just getting furniture now. Don't you think that's lazy?"

They walked toward the large furniture warehouse.

"We did. Leo and Pixie decided to have a big fight, and tada, they broke everything."

"Why aren't they buying?"

"They're fixing the damage to the actual clubhouse."

"I don't want to see that, do I?"

"You're not going to have much choice. We're dropping whatever we pick. You can help."

"I can?"

"Yep. If you decide pink and fluffy is what you want then we'll pick it up."

Grace laughed, linking her arm through his. "Are you sure about that? They'll beat the shit out of you."

"Nah, they won't. Well, they will, but I don't give a shit. I'll hold my own."

"Do you fight a lot?"

"I used to. Don't do it much anymore. I'm too old. When I'm really old, I'll probably suffer with it."

"Poor baby." She kissed his cheek, and it was all worth it. The blue balls and the wet dreams were all worth it for her kisses, and the sweet scent of strawberry coming from her.

"I am a poor baby."

They stayed linked as they started walking around the store.

Grace wasn't cruel, and she picked out some oak tables and chairs. Drake also picked out several of the style they already had. Together they decided on a pink fluffy love seat as punishment, which he'd make sure stayed in the main clubhouse.

In no time at all they were back in the car, and he stopped off at the pet store. He helped pick the bed, some toys, some food, and a carrying case.

"Are you sure you're ready for a pet?"

"No, not even close, but we can all love him. He's so cute, and he's white. Like a little ball of fluff. You'll see him. We've taken you up on the offer of giving us a ride."

"I'm pleased to be of service."

"You are."

Once her stuff was packed and resting in the passenger seat between them, they drove back to the clubhouse.

There was a small dumpster outside the doors, and the guys were still throwing shit away.

"Are you sure you don't want to drop me off first?"

"Babe, there's no way James would allow any of the brothers to fuck right now. He'd be so pissed."

They climbed out of the truck, and before he even started to unload the truck, he entered the clubhouse.

Pixie and Leo were at either end of the room, arguing, which he was surprised about.

"You shouldn't have started saying shit," Leo said.

"You're moping about the woman that's fucking the gym teacher. Just goes to show you and Paul don't have what it takes to keep a real woman."

"You can't even get a real woman to look at you, let alone have a single conversation," Leo shot back.

"That's it!" Pixie threw the brush down and walked toward Leo. Of course, Leo wouldn't back down, and James appeared in between.

"I will knock you both fucking down if you don't get back to business. You've cost the club a fucking fortune with your pansy ass complaining." James turned to Leo. "You couldn't keep Stacey because she was using you, just like she's using that other guy. Deal with it, get over it, and move on. She has, and she's not coming back." He then turned to Pixie, his brother. "Suzy won't even give you the time of day. She even eats in the kitchen with Teri so that she doesn't have to listen to you. You're not God's gift to women. You can't keep it in your pants, and you're never going to have a chance with Suzy. Get your head out of your ass."

Grace leaned in close. "I like him."

Drake burst out laughing. She liked everyone who put Pixie in his place. The other day she liked Thomas, who'd slammed his fist in Pixie's face for hitting on Sharon. It certainly had a lot of humor.

"Right, let's unload this crap."

With Grace's help, he unloaded the truck, carrying in pieces of furniture. When it came to the pink fluffy love seat, the guys tried to stop her from bringing it in, but he helped her.

"Every time you look at it, you'll remember this day," Grace said, dusting her hands together. The scent of the paint was too strong, so they left the clubhouse soon after their work was done.

"I'm so tired now," Grace said. "My arms ache."

"I enjoyed spending time together."

"Me too. It was fun."

When he dropped her off at the apartment, he didn't want to leave her, but he knew he didn't have much of a choice. It wouldn't be long until he was with her again. Drake lived for their time together.

****

"Come on, Drake, don't you think he's the cutest thing ever?" Grace said, holding out the white fluffy puppy they had bought. It was a Saturday morning, and she was off again. Her days changed every other week. Earlier that week, he'd gone with all three women to get the puppy. Of course, all he'd heard was about their new little dog that they had all called, Fluffy.

It was cute, he wouldn't lie.

"Look at that cutie face. You're so cute." Grace pressed a kiss to the pup's head and held him close. She moved toward Drake and placed the pup against his chest. "Here, hold him."

Drake held him in his hand, which was large enough for the pup to sit on. He held him close once Fluffy started to wriggle.

"Do you want a coffee?" she asked.

"I'd love one." He followed her into the kitchen, and Fluffy kept wriggling, so he put the pup down, letting him wander around. "Do you have to stay here all day?"

"No. We can take Fluffy out with us, or we can leave him here, but it's not really advised because he is a pup."

"How is he settling in?"

"He's so cute, and adorable. He's perfect, actually. He goes to bed, and he doesn't make much of a sound once he's there. He's a perfect little guy." Grace poured them both a coffee. "Are you getting pup broody?"

"Nope. If I got a dog it would be a German Shepherd, or a Rottweiler."

"Protection dogs?"

"You got it, babe."

"Seems a sad excuse to have a dog. Are the Dirty Fuckers in danger?" she asked.

Just hearing her say the word "fuck" had his cock pulsing, pressing against the front of his jeans. He was going to have to see a doctor or something. There was no way it was natural how many times he was getting hard, and they were lasting. He'd beat his dick until he was spent, but it was still fucking hard. He was in pain with how damn hard he was.

"All clubs are in danger. We like to protect our own."

She placed a coffee in front of him, adding sugar and cream just the way he liked it.

"I get that. I've seen some news about MCs in other towns. They're not all good."

"Some aren't, some are, and it depends how the Prez wants to run the club. James, he's a good Prez, and he has our best interests at heart. It's not just about the money to him."

"That's good." She sipped her drink. "So, what brings you here?"

"I was wondering if you'd like to come to the clubhouse for a barbeque. It will be above board, and I'll bring you home before anything goes crazy."

"When?"

"Tomorrow. Teri's going to be there, a few of the guys in town, obviously the brothers."

"Can Suzy and Chloe come?"

"You've gotten close to her, haven't you?"

"Chloe?"

"Yeah."

"Of course. What's not to like about her? She's so sweet, and charming, and adorable. Has she stopped by the club at all?" Grace asked.

"No. The brothers miss her." He knew Richard did as well. The lawyer visited the playrooms at the clubhouse, stayed to watch for an hour, and when there was no sign of Chloe, he left.

"I can imagine. I'd love to come. It would be fun, and like you said, there's no crazy stuff going down. I have to protect my eyeballs," she said.

He laughed. "You can even bring your little ball of fluff."

"Are you sure? We don't want him to get away."

"He'll be able to wander around, and there's an area we can pen off for him so he doesn't walk away."

"Excellent. Do I need to bring any food?"

"Nope, just yourself, and you don't even need to worry about that. I will drive you."

Grace grabbed her cell phone. "Let me just text the others, and see what they say."

He hoped Suzy and Chloe would go. If the two didn't go then Grace wouldn't go.

The cell phone beeped, and she smiled. "It's a party."

He would have fist pumped the air, but he decided that wasn't the right thing to do.

****

"Will Pixie be there?" Suzy asked.

"Probably. It's his club, but I doubt he'll do anything. Have you seen him recently?" Grace asked, pulling her hair up into a ponytail. She wore a pair of jeans and a summer vest top. It was really hot as Greater Falls was experiencing one of its heatwaves. Ice cream and freezing cold soda sales were on the rise, and hot, cooked meals were not. Teri adapted her menu to suit the mood, and she even had frozen yogurt or something cold mixed in for the breakfast menu. It was delicious.

Grace tried everything that Teri made, and she had gained a couple of pounds. When she was about to join a gym, Drake had stopped her, saying if she wanted to work out, he'd help her. At six in the morning, before her shift at the diner, he was at her apartment, dressed in running shorts, waiting for her.

She always wore baggy clothes so that he didn't see how big she actually was. They now ran in the morning together, and the more time she spent with Drake, the harder it was to put him in the friends category. They had a lunch date yesterday, and the night before that she'd had a sex dream about him, making it impossible to look at him.

"Are you okay?" Chloe asked.

Pulling out of her thoughts, she looked around the room to see that Suzy and Fluffy had disappeared. "Sorry, I was just inside my own head."

"Did your thoughts have anything to do with one very hunky biker?"

"Maybe." She smiled, and heat filled her cheeks. "I don't know. This thing with Drake, I'm getting a little afraid right now."

"Why?"

"He's just so, I don't know. I thought I could keep this friendship, and yet I can't."

"That's the way it always is. Drake wants you."

"I don't want to ruin this, Chloe. I like him, and we're friends. What if we try to do something, and I mess it up?" Grace asked.

"What makes you think *you'll* be the one to mess it up?"

"I'm always the one to mess things up. I couldn't even have a normal relationship."

Chloe held her hand up. "Loser Dwayne did not have a relationship with you. I don't care what you say. You've told me enough for me to know that he was using you. Drake, he's nothing like Dwayne."

"I don't want to ruin this."

"Maybe you won't ruin it. What if for a couple of

months, or years, you have something magical?"

"What if it ends?" Grace said.

"There are times that all good things must come to an end, honey. You're right, you and Drake, it could ruin your friendship, and for a short time the romance between the two of you may be explosive, but like all good shattering things, it's broken."

"You're not making me feel any better."

"Do you want to go through life being constantly afraid of feeling? You're terrified of finding love, and yet it's something we all need."

"You're miserable because of Richard."

"Again, that's my fault, not Richard's."

Grace took a deep breath. "You know what, I'm not going to be afraid of what hasn't happened."

"Don't live your life being afraid."

"Are you ready for this?" Suzy asked, coming out of her bedroom with Fluffy under her arm.

Before she could answer, the door sounded, and Chloe went to answer.

"Hello, ladies, are you ready to party?" Drake asked.

They all piled into Drake's car with Grace sitting at the front.

"Are you okay?" he asked.

"I'm great. You?"

"I'm doing good." He reached across the car, taking hold of her hand. She stared at their locked fingers, and her heart started to pound once again. When they were together, she had noticed that he spent a great deal of time finding any excuse to touch her. She loved his hands on her body, touching her, caressing her. Over the past few weeks, it was what she had come to enjoy.

In the back Chloe and Suzy were talking about the latest book they had been reading. Just lately, Chloe had been staying with Suzy as they read chapters to each other. Grace didn't feel left out as Drake had given her an e-reader as a gift, and filled it with hot, spicy romance. Did he know what kind of books he'd given her?

She didn't know if he did, or if it was all in her head. Grace had been the one to try to put their relationship in the friend zone, and now she didn't know what to do. Drake had started to invade little parts of her life, and she didn't know how to shut him out. More importantly, she didn't want to.

The clubhouse gate was open, and Drake parked the car nearest the gate so that they could leave when she wanted to. She found it charming that he was always being sweet to her.

He showed Suzy where to put Fluffy. Before they could put the little pup into the penned in area, Cora and several of the women came around, cooing over him.

"Fluffy is getting a lot more action than the guys," Drake said, whispering against her ear. "Do you fancy a beer?"

"I don't drink. A soda would be good." She followed him into the clubhouse, and at first the desire to close her eyes was strong, but she forced them open. The clubhouse didn't have many people inside. Most of them were all outside, drinking, and standing near a barbeque. She saw a lot of women in bikinis where their tits were bulging out.

"You can strip down if you want?" he said.

She burst out laughing. "You've got no chance of that happening. I'd make everyone sick."

"Don't do that," he said. "Don't put yourself down." He wrapped his arms around her, pressing her against the nearest wall.

"It's the truth."

"No, it's not."

Silence fell between them, and she saw that his gaze had fallen on her lips, and she couldn't help but lick them.

"Do you know what you're doing to me when you do that?" he asked.

"Drake?"

"It's getting harder, Grace."

He pressed his rock hard cock against her stomach, and she moaned, pressing her head to his.

They took a deep breath, and slowly, they withdrew. Drake took her hand, and they grabbed a couple of sodas for themselves.

Together, they walked out into the yard, and Grace leaned against Drake's arm, watching the men of the Dirty Fuckers, wondering if she was losing her mind by wanting to be with him. She saw that Cora was dancing with James. The tension between Grace and Drake were mounting, and she only hoped they didn't lose each other in the process.

Chapter Eight

Two weeks later

Drake sat down beside Grace as she had almost passed out on their running trail. It was seven at night, and the sun was setting.

"I feel like I'm going to throw up. Please tell me my ass looks a little smaller." She rolled over, pushing her ass out.

He laughed, slapping her ass, and rubbing the sore spot.

"I'm too tired to hurt you back." She rested her head against her arms, and he heard her breathing deeply. "Why did I want to do this?"

"I don't know. You're the one that was convinced your ass is huge. I could inspect." He ran his hand over her ass, feeling her softness. His cock pressed against the front of his shorts, and he didn't even try to hide it.

"Drake?" She released a moan, and he moved in close.

Grace turned her head to look at him.

"I'm seeing where there's too much fat? I like this, baby. I can't see where there's any fat." He gave her ass a squeeze, and she pressed her ass against his hand.

"We need to stop."

He moved his hand to the top of her thigh, moving up and down. She opened her thighs a little wider, and he couldn't resist. He slipped his finger against her pussy, teasing her.

She gasped and lifted herself up, giving him better access to her pussy. Cupping her completely, he felt how wet she was.

Grace moved, turning, and her gaze was on his. Her cheeks flushed. In the distance they heard the rustling of the trees. Taking her hand, he placed it over his bulging cock. "That's what you do to me, babe."

"This will change us."

"You've felt this change coming for some time now. You felt it long before the night of the party. This is how it's supposed to be between us." He cupped her cheek, sliding his fingers down to her neck, over her collarbone. The shorts were loose, and he pressed his thumb against her cunt, feeling the lips of her sex spread. She squeezed his cock, running her fingers up and down his shaft. "I've been wandering what it would be like to fuck you, Grace, to spread you out, and take you so fucking hard that you're screaming my name." Staring at her lips, he saw that she was biting her bottom lip. He wanted to bite that lip, to suck it between his teeth, and hear her moaning his name as she came from his fingers deep inside her. "Don't fight it."

Leaning in, he claimed her lips, running his tongue across her bruised flesh, sliding inside her mouth. She moaned, opening up to him. She rubbed her pussy against his hands, begging him with her body for more.

Moving his hand up, he pushed into her shorts, touching her through her panties, which were damp. The scent of her pussy teased his nostrils, and he wanted to taste her. This was not the place for him to lick her, but soon, he would.

He couldn't wait another second and so he ran his fingers through her creamy slit.

"Baby, you're soaking wet," he said.

"Drake? I'm scared."

"Don't be scared. There's no reason to be scared. I'm here. Do you want me to stop?" He'd stop if she wanted him to, and if she couldn't stand for him to actually touch her.

"We're friends."

"We can be more."

He wanted so damn much for there to be more.

Slowly, he stroked through her slit, watching her breath catch. The shirt she wore pressed close to her body, and he got a good look at her juicy tits. The nipples were rock hard, and it didn't have anything to do with the warm air. There wasn't a single breeze in the warm night.

"Let your body feel, Grace. I'm not Dwayne. I'm not someone looking for my own pleasure. Just you."

Her hand moved from his cock, grabbing his shirt. She tugged it over his head, and he threw it down beside them. They were in a secluded part of the running course, and it was also late so no one was going to stumble upon them. He grabbed her shirt from her and started to pull it up. She didn't fight him, and he was gutted at the fact he couldn't see her body clearly.

The outline of her sports bra let him know it was as ugly as all other sports bras. He was going to by her some lacy stuff so that she could strip in front of him. She sat up, pulling the sports bra over her head.

This was happening, finally. He was going to be inside her, and know how tight her cunt was.

He stood, dropping his shorts, and wrapping his hands around his cock. Going to his knees, he pushed her down gently, and took over. "Let me, baby."

Drake pulled her baggy shorts down her thighs, and then spread her open. He'd taken her panties off along with the shorts. Cupping her pussy, he slid a finger inside her and groaned. Her pussy was so fucking tight that she clenched onto his finger. In and out, he moved inside her wet pussy, wanting his dick inside her.

Removing his fingers from her cunt, he flicked her clit.

"I want to hear you come before I fuck you."

"I don't think I can. I never could before."

"I'm not just any fucking man, baby. This is me, and I want you to hear you scream my name as you come." He was going to hear her scream before he even got inside her.

The sun fell behind them, and Drake plunged two fingers inside her tight pussy, using his thumb to tease her clit.

Claiming her mouth, he took her lips in a deep, searing kiss, swallowing down her screams. Grace thrust against his fingers, making him go inside her, touching her clit a little more firmly. Kissing down to her neck, he sucked onto her pulse, and then moved down, taking one of her nipples into his mouth. Her nipples were large, and he flicked the tip with his tongue before sucking it in. He bit down hard, and she screamed his name. She tightened as he drew her orgasm from her body.

She cried out his name, and as she came apart, he smiled.

"That's it, baby. Give it all to me."

Only when she came down from her orgasm did he pull his fingers out of her. Licking her cum, he loved her taste, knowing he was going to have his face between her thighs at the first opportunity.

Gripping his cock, he moved between her thighs, rubbing the head between her slit. He rubbed her clit, coating his dick in her cream.

"Please, Drake," she said.

"It's okay, baby." Sliding down, he eased the tip inside her cunt, and gritted his teeth. She was so damn tight.

Pushing an inch inside her, he heard Grace wince. "You're a lot bigger than Dwayne."

"Babe, I love that I'm bigger than your ex, but I don't need to know that while I'm here."

Pushing another inch inside her, he rested his hand on the ground, and slammed every single inch of his cock deep inside her.

She screamed out, and so she didn't draw any possible attention to them, he claimed her lips, silencing her sounds.

Her pussy clenched around his cock, each spasm making it hard for him to control his own desire. It had been well over a month since he'd been inside a woman, and his control was only so good. He wanted to fuck her, to take her, and ravish her pussy so there wasn't any other person she could think of.

"Drake? I need you, please."

Resting his head against hers, Drake counted to ten. He may want to fuck her, but he wasn't going to hurt her. Her ex had made a habit of giving her bad sex. He was going to be the complete opposite, and give her something a hell of a lot better.

When she started to wriggle on his cock, Drake couldn't hold back any longer. Pulling out of her cunt, he stared down. Groaning in frustration as he couldn't see, he slammed all the way back inside her.

"The next time I have you, baby, we're going to have the light on, and I'm going to watch my cock slide in and out of you."

"Drake, God, it feels so good."

Taking possession of her lips, he fucked her hard against the dirt, not caring if anyone came by to stop them. He slid his cock in and out of her, wishing he could see. He'd have her on her knees so that he could see her beautiful pussy and asshole, and he could decide between either one.

"This body, baby, it belongs to me. No one else." Kissing her neck, he moved down to her pulse, biting down.

He pounded inside her going deep.

"I'm going to come."

"Then come, Grace, let me feel your pussy soak my dick. Come on, baby."

Slamming inside her, he didn't give up or relent, thrusting deep. Her pussy was far better than anything he ever imagined. She was so soft and tight.

"Yes, Drake, please."

"Fuck, baby, so damn tight and hot."

Grace screamed his name, and her pussy tightened around him. She came all over his cock, and he felt the rush of her sweet cream surround him.

Unable to hold back, he fucked her harder, pressing every single inch within her, until he came, spilling his seed inside her.

It was the greatest moment of his life, and when he collapsed, he wrapped his arms around Grace, promising himself he was never going to let go.

****

Grace let herself into her apartment and was as quiet as she could be. Suzy's door was closed, and there was no sign of Chloe or of Fluffy. Locking the door, she tiptoed across the floor paying careful attention not to make a sound. The last thing she wanted to deal with was an inquisition from her friends.

Entering her room, she saw it was clear and grabbed her pajamas. Tiptoeing across the apartment, she entered the bathroom, closing the door, and running herself a bath. While the water ran, she glanced in the mirror and winced. Her hair was covered in dry dirt, and her clothes were a mess. Removing the clothes, she saw her back wasn't much better.

After Drake had fucked her, they had heard another couple heading toward them. There hadn't been time to talk, or to laugh with each other. They had grabbed their clothing and moved along. Of course, Drake had been curious about who had invaded their space, and they'd seen it was James and Cora. The couple ended up screwing in pretty much the exact same spot that they had been seconds before. Moving away from the spot quietly, Drake had driven her home, promising to see her tomorrow at the diner.

Have I just made the biggest mistake of my life?
She didn't know how to answer that.

Lying in the water, she stared up at the ceiling, thinking about how good it felt to have his cock sliding in and out of her. She cupped her pussy, sliding her fingers inside her soreness. Closing her eyes, she had to bite her lip to stop herself from moaning out.

Jerking her hands away, she shook her head. Their one time together had been worth more than the hundreds of times Dwayne had taken her. She didn't want to think of her ex, or in any way compare him to Drake. By far, Drake was the better between the two men.

Washing her body, she hurried up cleaning away the dirt that had clung to her skin. Drake was the first person she'd rolled around with in the dirt.

Stepping out of the bath, she wrapped a towel around her body and cleaned out the tub before padding back to her room. Closing the door, she dried her body, pulling on some shorts and a vest, and was about to start brushing her hair when a noise made her scream. Turning around, she saw Chloe sitting in her bed. The other woman had turned the light on.

"What are you doing here? I was here a second ago, and you weren't here."

"I heard you come in, and then I heard the unmistakable sound of tiptoeing. I got curious and wanted to know what would have you sneaking into your own apartment. You do realize you're an adult. Sneaking is the thing of the past?"

Dropping the brush against her side, Grace stared at her friend. "I didn't want to have to talk about it."

"You did something naughty?"

"Naughty, stupid, wrong. I don't know what way to describe it. It's after nine, Suzy was in bed, and I didn't want to have to talk about it."

"What happened?" Chloe asked.

"See, this is why I tried to sneak in here."

"Okay, point taken." Chloe turned out the lights, lying back down in her bed. "Goodnight."

Brushing her hair, Grace gritted her teeth. All she wanted to do now was talk about it.

Once she was finished, she climbed into bed, and turned over to stare at Chloe, whose eyes were closed.

"I slept with Drake."

Chloe's eyes opened. "Slept with or fucked?"

"There's a difference?"

"Yep, to the club, slept with means no action actually happened. Fucked, action indeed happened."

"You've spent too much time with that club."

"In a way, they're my family. So you slept with or fucked Drake?"

"I fucked Drake, or he fucked me—there was fucking involved."

Chloe giggled. "I think it's sweet when you do shit like that. Say the same word over and over, trying to justify it."

"I'm not trying to justify it. I don't know what I'm trying to do."

"Did you enjoy it?" Chloe asked.

"Yes, I did. I loved it."

"You were at the clubhouse?"

"No. We, erm, we did it outside." Grace covered

her face. "I sound like a slut."

"I've done it outside."

"Not a slut then?"

Chloe started laughing. "You really need to stop worrying about what people think. Did you enjoy it?"

"I loved it."

"Then what are you going to do about it?"

"I've not got the faintest idea. I'm scared."

"About what?"

"What if this changes us?"

"I doubt that."

"How can you know?"

Chloe sighed. "You and Drake are the same people. Nothing has changed between you, not really."

"I don't know if we are."

"Do you no longer want to hang out with him?" Chloe asked.

"I do."

"Then what is the problem? You'll just have a lot more to do other than dinner, running, the movies."

"Do you really think it's possible to have both? Friendship and sex?"

"The Dirty Fuckers are my friends, and I've fucked them. I'm not suffering for it."

"But you're here because of that guy, that lawyer guy hurting you. You're in love with him. How can that not hurt?"

Chloe was silent. "Drake is not like Richard. They're two completely different people, and you can't compare the two."

"Have you ever thought of talking to Richard?" Grace hated to see her friend hurting. Chloe deserved so much better. She was such a sweet woman, and not many people saw it, but she put others' needs before her own.

"I've tried to talk to him. He's not interested in

talking to me. He just wants to dominate me, and that's not the only thing I'm interested in." She stuck her bottom lip out. Grace reached toward said lip and tugged, stopping the action.

"Don't cry."

"It hurts, Grace. I've seen him in town with other women, and seeing him hurts. I feel like I'm being torn in two, and it's all my fault."

Wrapping her arms around Chloe, she waited as Chloe sobbed against her shoulder. "Why is it all your fault?"

"Because of who I am. I'm a whore."

Capturing her chin, Grace forced Chloe to look at her. "Don't call yourself that. Never call yourself that."

"It's what the men call me. I'm a club whore. I'm not some old lady."

"That's not who you are on the inside. You didn't fuck anyone outside of the club, did you?"

"No."

"Then you're club property. You're not anyone else's property," she said. Grace had been around Drake long enough to know the difference between club property and not. "If Richard can't see your loyalty then he's not worth your time, and you shouldn't worry about him. He's an asshole."

"I wish I hadn't fallen in love with an asshole."

"I know, honey. They don't say love is easy."

"Do you love Drake?"

"I don't know. I care about him, and sometimes I'm so nervous in case this all goes wrong."

"If it goes wrong you still have us. Life is about having fun, and all we're doing is dealing with the possible heartbreak." Chloe chuckled.

There was a knock at the door, and Grace shouted for Suzy to enter.

"Do you know how late it is?" Suzy asked.

Grace glanced across at the clock to see it was just after nine. "Seriously? That's not late."

"I've not been sleeping well lately." Suzy held Fluffy in her arms, and Grace moved over to give some space for her friend.

Suzy sat down, and Fluffy curled up in a ball on the bed.

"Why haven't you been sleeping?" she asked.

"Pixie came to the shop earlier this week, and he brought a woman with him."

"Why is that stopping you from sleeping?" Chloe asked.

"Yeah, I thought you hated Pixie."

"I do hate him. He was still trying to ask me out, and I was helping the woman he'd brought with him. When he went off to look for something else, the woman told me in no uncertain terms that my fat ass would never make it in the club, that the women would tear me apart." Suzy sighed. "Why do women have to be so mean to each other?"

"I don't know. We've got each other."

"Kitty Cat is the nicest woman in the club. Everyone else, they're wanting to get one of the men to make them as an old lady." Chloe snuggled up. "What they don't understand is the men are never going to marry them, or make them an old lady."

"You really believe that, don't you?" Grace asked.

"They're not going to allow it to happen. The men, they like to have a woman to call their own," Chloe said.

"This sucks. We're all talking about what men do and don't want. They should accept women how they come."

"It's not like there's a lot of competition for me. I've not had sex with anyone," Suzy said. "I don't even care about what I'm missing."

Grace chuckled. "You're going to love it when it happens."

"I thought you said it sucked."

"It does, with the wrong man."

"You finally did it with the right man?" Suzy asked.

Grace nodded.

"Drake?"

"Yes."

Suzy gave a little squeal. "I wondered when that was going to happen. Tell me all about it."

Rolling her eyes, Grace told her friend exactly what happened, and by the end of it, they were all lying down on the bed, sighing.

"I want to have sex," Suzy said. "That sounds so amazing."

"Pixie is an easy lay. He's guaranteed to give you what you want."

"I know, but then he'd be smug."

"Not if you use him, and then you walk away. Pixie is used to women hanging around his neck. You can use him, and walk away, then pretend it never happened, which would be cool. Pixie has a massive ego, and the guys would love for him to be pulled down a peg or two."

"I don't know. I want to have sex, not give a guy something to brag about."

"The one thing the men won't do is brag unless you're a club whore, and share the guys," Chloe said. "Pixie won't say a thing."

Grace stared up at the ceiling. She wondered what Drake was doing. Was he thinking about what happened between them? She looked forward to seeing him again, and was also nervous about it.

MY KIND OF DIRTY

Chapter Nine

Drake walked around the clothing racks, and he couldn't for the life of him find what he was looking for. Grace hadn't talked to him, or messaged him, and he'd not gone to the diner either. Last night had been the best experience of his life, and he'd fucked a lot of woman, and now he didn't want to screw this up.

He saw Suzy putting out more clothes, and he cleared his throat to get her attention.

"Drake, what are doing here?" Suzy asked, moving toward him.

"I want to buy something for Grace, but I don't have a clue what to get her."

"You want to buy clothes for her?" Suzy frowned, looking at the clothing that he'd picked out. It was for running gear, and he shook his head.

"No."

"Then what do you want to get her?"

He glanced over her shoulder toward the underwear, and Suzy looked behind her.

"Drake, if you want to get her some underwear, then get her some underwear," Suzy said.

"I'm buying it for Grace."

"Okay."

"You know that right?"

"I'm really confused now, Drake. What's the problem? I'm not going to tease you or start telling everyone that you've bought underwear." She frowned at him.

"I don't want you telling Grace that I was buying underwear in case she thinks it's for someone else."

"Oh, in case I made her think that you were cheating."

"Which I'm not. I'm buying stuff for Grace."

Suzy placed her hand over her mouth and chuckled. "You're seriously overthinking this, Drake. I wouldn't have even thought that you were buying stuff for someone else." She looked past him toward the counter. "I've got to go and serve some customers. Buy what you want."

She left him alone, shaking her head.

He really didn't want to screw this up with Grace, and already he was nervous as fuck.

Get your fucking head in the game!

Moving toward the underwear, he started looking through the variety that was on offer. Lace, silk, padded, low cut, and there were even some sexy ones that held the breasts up, showing off the nipples.

Thinking about Grace's dark brown hair and pale skin, he started to pick some pastel color, along with a set of red, and even white lace. He wanted to see her dark nipples peeking through the white lace, along with the dark hair covering her pussy.

He was getting hard just thinking about it.

"What are you doing here?" Pixie asked, making Drake jump.

"What the fuck, man?" Drake figured he had enough to get started, and glared at his brother. "Why are you here?"

"I always come here."

"He does. He's made it his own personal hobby, haven't you, Pixie?" Suzy asked, coming to stand with them. "You just can't get rid of him."

"Promise to go out with me, and I'll give you a break."

"So one date is all it will take for you to lose interest?"

"Not interest, but I'll give you time to get over what I'd do to your pussy."

Suzy laughed. "Whatever." She turned toward Drake. "Did you find what you want?"

"I did. I'm ready to leave now."

He followed Suzy back to the counter, and she rang up his purchases. Drake noticed she kept on looking toward Pixie, and sometimes she'd bite her lip before shaking her head, and finishing off.

"Is everything okay?" he asked.

"Yeah, of course, why wouldn't it be?"

"You're looking at Pixie a little conflicted."

"It's nothing. I was just thinking about a conversation Chloe, Grace, and I were having. Don't worry about it."

He paid the bill and took the small bag she handed to him. "Grace finishes work at twelve today, right?"

"Yes. It's her half day, and Chloe's working until seven, and I finish here at around five. If you want the apartment free, you've got between when you get her home from twelve, until about five-thirty or six, depending on traffic."

"You're pimping out your friend?" he asked.

"Not at all. I'm hoping Grace has a lot of fun."

"See you around, Suzy."

He left the shop and made his way toward his bike. Riding out to the clubhouse, he found Caleb working on his bike. The brother didn't have a shirt on, and every now and then, he looked toward the single swing that they had built between two large trees. Kitty Cat was sitting on it, swinging forward and back. Her gaze looked completely blank.

"Is everything okay with her?"

"It should be. She's just having a rough time dealing with some of her memories. Last night I didn't work her hard enough before she went to bed." Caleb looked troubled as he stared off at the woman who meant the world to him. "She found out that I shared Cora with James."

"Does it bother her?"

"I don't know. She's acting like it doesn't, but I'm not so sure."

"How long do you think you can keep this up?" Drake asked.

"What?"

"Don't give me that. You and I both know that Kitty Cat is your woman. No other brother touches her. She flirts, and there's some light foreplay, but before it goes any further, they stop it."

Drake had never fucked Kitty Cat. He'd watched her getting spanked, and Caleb working her hard in the playroom, but he'd never actually fucked the woman. Kitty Cat wouldn't allow Caleb to handle her aftercare either. Most of the time after a Dom and sub scene, the Dom provided the sub with aftercare, bringing her down slowly and carefully. Kitty wouldn't allow Caleb to do that, so they experienced moments where she didn't seem to be there.

"She's not talking to me right now."

"I'm grabbing my car, and heading toward the diner. I'll let you handle whatever shit you're dealing with." Drake wasn't going to get involved with whatever trouble was coming Caleb's way. That kind of shit was private.

Leaving his bike, he grabbed his car, and headed out toward the diner. Leaving the underwear inside the car, he entered, calling out a greeting to Teri.

Sitting at the main counter, he watched as Grace moved around the room. Her hair was pulled into a ponytail, and he stared down the length of her back. He'd been inside her sweet pussy, and his cock hardened even more.

Grace saw him and paused. Her cheeks heated, and he just knew she was thinking about his cock sliding in and out of her.

"Hey," she said, moving toward him.

"Hello, beautiful."

She rounded the counter, and she licked her lips. "What can I get for you?"

"I'll take a stack of pancakes and a coffee."

She wrote the order down on her pad and placed it on the order spinner. He saw Teri come get his order, giving him a wink as she did.

The coffee was placed in front of him, exactly how he liked it.

"I was expecting you to come in earlier," she said.

"I had to do a little shopping. I've got plans for you at twelve."

"Plans?"

"Yes. I'm taking you back to your apartment, and I've got you a little something I want you to try on."

Grace smiled. "You're being a little evasive."

"You're going to love it."

"I am?"

"Yes."

"I look forward to it." She looked over his shoulder, and excused herself. He watched her walking away, admiring the full curves her butt. His cock had a mind of its own, and he was pleased he was sitting down.

"Here you go, honey," Teri said, putting the plate of pancakes in front of him. "You're looking pretty happy today."

"I am."

"So is Grace."

Drake took a bite of his pancake, which Teri had

already drenched in maple syrup.

"Has Grace told you something?"

"Not at all. I looked at you, and then I looked at Grace, putting two things together. It was good, wasn't it?"

"Shut up, Teri."

"What? I'm not allowed to be damn happy for my friend? I think it's awesome. You and Grace getting it on." Teri chuckled. "I knew you two would make a cute couple, and that whole friendship thing wouldn't last."

Drake shook his head. "Whatever."

"Don't hurt her, Drake."

"I have no plan to hurt her. I'm going to take care of her."

"Good. I'd hate to have to come after you. Grace deserves a man to show her how good it can be."

She gave him a wink and left to go back into the kitchen. He had a lot of plans to keep Grace's smile on her face.

****

Suzy stared at Pixie, thinking about what Chloe had said. She was still a virgin, and she had read a lot of erotic romance, and even watched a lot of porn. She wanted to experience sex, but she didn't want it to be a fleeting one night stand with a half-drunk man.

"I can feel you thinking all the way over here," Pixie said.

He was reading a newspaper. She wondered if any of the club knew he had a tendency to camp out at the shop, reading.

"Don't you have a clubhouse or something to hang out at?" she asked.

"I do, but here I like the peace and quiet."

"The women are all over you here."

"I have moments like this when it's quiet." He

closed the newspaper and stared at her. "Are you trying to have a real conversation with me?"

"Not at all." She pretended to clear away her desk.

"At the club there's always something to do. Fix a bike, fetch shit, deal with bitches arguing, helping out at the diner, looking over legal documents, it's all there waiting to be dealt with."

"You deal with it?" she asked.

"Not all of it, but I have my fair share."

"So, you're coming here to be a slob, and lazy."

"I come here because I like looking at the woman who won't give me the time of day, and it's nice, it's peaceful, and I don't have to deal with a bitch wanting to ride my cock all day, or to prove that she can get me deeper down her throat."

Suzy blushed. Pixie had always been blunt. She should be used to it by now, yet she wasn't.

"That's a colorful description."

"Believe me, I'm not fucking bragging, not by a long shot. I was sitting with two women in front of me. My dick in one woman's mouth, and they were more interested in who could do better. It was boring."

Huge mistake thinking Pixie could be the one.

"You know what, I really don't need to know anymore. You've gotten quite detailed, and stuff like that I don't need to know."

Pixie sighed, and Suzy moved toward the dressing rooms, and started to straighten the clothes, before taking them back to their place on the racks.

He stepped right up beside her. "Are you going to tell me why you've been eye-fucking me all morning?" he asked.

Suzy tensed up. "You're awfully close."

"And you've done nothing but think about

fucking since I got here."

"No, I haven't," she lied.

"Yes. You have. Your nipples are pressing against your shirt, and the bra you're wearing doesn't do shit to hide the fact you want me." He cupped her breast, and heat filled her pussy. She closed her eyes, pressing her breast into his hand. "Tell me what you want."

"No."

"If you don't tell me, I don't know if I can give it to you."

Suzy pulled out of his grip and turned to stare at him. She wanted to order him, to instruct him, and instead, she chickened out. "There's nothing I want."

Moving away from him, she mentally cursed herself as she continued working.

****

"We're going back to my apartment," Grace said.

Chloe had swapped places with her at the diner, and she knew Suzy was working until late. The apartment, it was going to be free most of the afternoon.

"There's something I want you to do for me." Drake took hold of her hand as they rode toward the apartment building. Her pussy was soaking wet as she imagined what he wanted from her. She tried not to think about it in case he wanted something completely different from her, and she had misread the signals.

She really hoped that wasn't the case.

"I enjoyed last night," Grace said, then cringed. What kind of person said that?

Drake chuckled. "I fucking loved last night, and you know what, it's not going to be the last time either."

"It's not?"

"Do you think you can get enough of me from one night only?"

"Your ego needs some work."

"My ego is exactly where I need him to be."

"I don't believe it, not for a second." Grace leaned over, and kissed his cheek. "I don't want our friendship to disappear."

"It's not going to. I'm not using you for a fuck, Grace."

She felt a lot better for him saying that.

When they got to her apartment, he parked the car, and she waited while he grabbed a paper bag from the back of the car. They used the elevator, and for her the tension between them seemed be getting thicker.

Drake took the keys from her and quickly bent down to scoop up Fluffy.

"I love you, Fluff, but this afternoon, you're spending the day in Momma Suzy's room."

Closing the door, she watched him put the pup inside Suzy's room, closing the door. "That was mean."

"I want the afternoon with my girl." He removed his leather jacket. "Take your clothes off."

"Strip? You want me to strip?"

"Yep." He poured different colored fabrics onto the couch. "I bought these for you."

"You didn't have to buy me anything."

"Then consider that I bought these for myself so that I could see my woman in them."

"Your woman?"

He moved in close, wrapping his arm around her waist. "Yes, my woman. That's exactly what you are, mine." Drake slammed his lips down on hers, and Grace moaned. She locked her arms around his neck, pressing her body against his. "Fuck, baby, you feel so good."

Drake pulled away, unbuttoning her blouse.

She patted his hands away. "I can do it, if you really want me to."

"I do." He moved away, going to the pile of

underwear. It was the first time that anyone had ever bought her something so personal.

"I want you to try these on first."

He held up a dark red lacy pair.

She stood in her plain white underwear. The panties she wore had love hearts on them, and they had to be the most unattractive thing she could have bought.

"Please pretend that you didn't see these," she said.

"Don't worry. Try these on."

Taking the underwear he offered, she was about to go to her room, but Drake stopped her.

"I want to watch." He pulled the single seat around so that he was facing her.

"You want to watch me try on underwear?"

"Yes, every single piece."

"O-okay." Removing her bra, her cheeks heated, and she tried not to think of Drake watching her in awful looking underwear.

She put on the red lacy pair, and the moment she put the bra in place and the panties rested against her hips, she felt a difference. They were so soft and beautiful.

"Turn for me."

Grace did as he instructed, turning this way and that.

"Give me your back, and bend over."

"I'm not doing that."

"When we're done, I intend to bend you over right here, and fuck you from behind. Don't be shy, baby."

Biting her lip, she bent over at the waist, showcasing her ass to him.

"Fuck, baby."

After that, he kept on handing her different colors

of lace and silk. Each new outfit had her blushing even more.

At the end, he picked a white lacy set, and Drake stood moving toward her. She stood against the wall, licking her lips as she stared at him.

"Every time you lick your lips, I imagine them wrapped around my cock."

At those words, she couldn't help but think about his cock in her mouth.

"You ever sucked a man's cock before?"

"No."

"Do you want to suck mine?"

"Yes, I do."

He unhooked his jeans, kicked his boots off, and pushed his jeans down his thighs. Heat spilled from the lips of her pussy. She was so aroused.

"Get on your knees, baby. I want to give you a chance to experience everything."

Wrapping her fingers around his cock, she squeezed his cock a little tighter. He groaned, and she released him quickly. "Did I hurt you?"

"No, babe."

Staring at the tip of his large cock, she saw that there was a jewel of cum at the tip. She flicked her tongue against the tip, and tasted him.

"Fuck, baby. Do you like the taste of me?"

"Yes."

Covering the tip with her mouth, she sucked the head into her mouth then slid down his shaft until he hit the back of her throat.

"You can use your teeth if you want, baby."

She was gentle as she scored her teeth along the shaft, moving up. Glancing up at him, she watched as he closed his eyes, biting his lip.

Focusing on his dick, she started to bob on the

tip, and he seemed to be getting a little harder as she took more of him in her mouth. Pre-cum spilled out of the tip, and she swallowed it down.

"Fuck, baby, your mouth is so perfect, so fucking perfect."

He tugged the band out of her hair, and she let out a gasp at the sharp pain.

Releasing his cock, she stared up at him.

"Do you like my dick?"

"Yes."

"Good." Drake wrapped her hair around his fist, and gripped his cock. "Open for me, baby."

She opened her lips, staring into his eyes as he slid his cock into her mouth. "Um," she said, moaning around his dick.

"Fuck, I'm not going to last."

He started to ease in and out of her, going deep. When he hit the back of her throat, he pulled away, and he set up a steady pace, pumping into her mouth.

"Yes, fuck, baby. Fuck, fuck, fuck, fuck, fuck."

His words encouraged her to take him deeper into his mouth, swallowing the tip.

"No, I'm not going to last."

He pulled on her hair so she had no choice but to get to her feet. He moved her toward the couch, pushing her down.

Grace didn't have time to ask him what he was doing. He pushed her back, removed the white lace panties, and spread her open. His fingers eased the lips of her pussy open, and Grace cried out as he sucked her clit into his mouth. Drake didn't stay there for long. He moved down, plunging his tongue into her pussy, and using his fingers to tease her clit.

He was all over her body, and she couldn't believe how good it was. He finger-fucked her several

times before moving up to caress her clit.
"Yes, Drake, so good."
Drake used his teeth biting on her nub. His fingers thrust inside her, and he stretched her wide.
"Come for me, Grace."
She came hard as he flicked her clit with his tongue and fucked inside her with his fingers.
The pleasure was out of this world, and she came hard, spilling her cream onto his fingers.
Drake didn't give her the chance to come down from her arousal, and he stood, grabbing her arms, and bending her over the end of the couch.
"What are you doing?" she asked.
"Taking what belongs to me."
His cock pressed against her entrance, and in one thrust, he was deep inside her. Drake wasn't a small man, and she cried out his name as he pounded deep into her.
"Fuck, baby, you've got no idea how damn sweet you feel. Your pussy is perfect, so tight and wet. I'm going to have to fuck you over and over again until you remember me."
She wouldn't complain.
He gripped her hips, and started to work in and out, making her feel every inch of his dick sliding inside her. He took his time, and the pleasure had her gasping for more.
"I love fucking your pussy."
With each word he pounded inside her.
"Yes, Drake. Fuck me."
"Who do you belong to?"
"You."
"That's right, baby. My pussy, my ass, my tits, they all belong to me, and no other man is going to know what it's like to be inside you."
She screamed her agreement.

He held her hips so tightly she knew he was going to leave bruises. She would be more than happy with his marks on her skin.

As he slammed deep inside her, she pushed back, fucking him harder.

Nothing was gentle in their fucking.

It was hard, hungry, and desperate.

"I'm going to come," he said.

In the next second, she heard him cry out her name, and felt the kick of his cock as he pulsed inside her, spilling his seed deep.

Taking deep breaths, Grace started to remember something really important.

"We've not used a condom." They had had sex twice now, and both times they hadn't used a condom.

MY KIND OF DIRTY

Chapter Ten

Two days later

Drake kept hold of Grace's hand as they moved through the large forest in Vale Valley. This was the area of the Trojans, and he didn't want to have a problem with the other biker gang. He didn't want them to be interrupted, and he'd visited this lake many times.

"Why aren't you wearing your leather cut?" Grace asked.

So far they had stolen moments with each other to be together. They'd had dinner together, and Grace had even cooked for him. Suzy and Chloe had been there. She wasn't comfortable going to the clubhouse, and with her friends living with her, they hadn't had sex unless it was behind the back of the diner.

He was getting tired of behaving like a naughty teenager.

"We're in a different MC's territory, and I don't want to cause any problems."

"Why travel all this way?"

"You're not comfortable around the clubhouse, and we don't have places of our own. This is the only place I can think for us to go that will give us some privacy."

"I can't afford a place of my own," Grace said.

He held a large picnic basket, and when he found a secluded area with enough shade from the trees, with a perfect view of the lake, he stopped. Drake heard in the distance far up the embankment the sound of kids, but he wasn't worried. During his many visits to the lake in Vale Valley, he'd not been found out by any of the Trojans.

The last thing he wanted to do was start a

possible war between the two clubs. Dirty Fuckers were not about war, but if posed with a possible threat, they would fight.

"You don't want to come to my room at the clubhouse either." He removed the blanket, putting it on the ground.

"Would you like me to come to your room?" Grace asked, biting her lip.

He stared up at her, and saw she was a little uncertain about what was happening.

Moving in front of her, he cupped her face, kissing her deeply. "I'd love you to come to my room." Stroking down her neck, he rested the tips of his fingers on her pulse. "You've got nothing to be afraid of."

"I know that."

"Do you? Do you really? I don't think you do. No one will touch you."

"I've never been around that kind of thing."

"That kind of thing? Why don't you try it? Come to the club Friday night."

"You want me to come to the club?" she asked.

"Yeah, come to the club. I'll give you a tour. We'll have a little fun, and then we can go to my room, and I can fuck your brains out without having to worry about your roommates hearing us." He stole a kiss, happy when she tried to deepen it. "Take your dress off."

Grace's face heated, and she looked around them.

"There's no one here, baby."

"You're always trying to get me naked."

Removing his shirt, he kicked off his boots, and his jeans. "Join me." He ran and jumped into the lake. The water was warm, and when he broke the surface, he saw her laughing. "Jump in."

"No, you've got no chance."

"Come on. It feels great."

"No."

"I'll lick your pussy until you come all over my face."

"Drake?"

"And then I'll do it all over again."

"Will you do that thing with your fingers?"

Drake chuckled. "Yes." He'd been playing with her ass every chance he got. He wanted to fuck her ass, and watch her come.

Grace removed her dress, kicking off her pumps, and running toward the lake. She screamed seconds before she hit the water. He waited for her to break the surface, pulling her into his arms, and turning her around.

"Hey, baby."

"This feels so good," she said.

"And we're alone. No one is here." He ran his hands up and down her body. "So, you'll come to the party?"

"Yes, I'll come to the party. Teri always looks happy after being at one of the parties. What should I wear?" she asked.

"How about I buy you something to wear?"

"What if I don't like it?"

"From what I've seen you wear you're not going to have anything suitable." Grace averted her gaze, and he cupped her cheek, forcing her to look at him. "What is it?"

"Nothing."

"Don't keep any secrets from me."

"Not ever?"

"No, not ever."

Grace sighed. "The club women. They're not going to like me."

"Babe, they don't even like Cora, but they put up with her because she's James's old lady, and they don't have a choice. Also, Cora would totally kick their ass if any of them even tried something."

"Cora sounds like a hard ass."

"She really is. Did you hear what she said to Stacey?"

"I was surprised. They're friends, right?"

"They are friends, but Cora's James's old lady, and she has to think of the club as well."

"Stacey hasn't come into the diner, and when I've seen her around town, she's no longer with Bill, the gym teacher. I hear he's with Misty."

"That woman is bad news."

"I agree. I don't like Misty." Grace moved away from him, swimming in little circles. "This is a little piece of heaven, isn't it?"

"Yes."

"Does this mean I'm your old lady?" Grace asked.

"That was something I wanted to ask you," Drake said. He kept himself afloat, watching her. "If you're coming to one of the parties, I want you to come as my old lady."

Grace smiled. "I'm going to be your old lady."

"Yep."

"You're my old man."

"You did accuse me of being old."

Grace laughed. "Totally hot kind of old." She winked at him, and moved to him again, wrapping her arms around his neck. "I would totally love to be your old lady."

"Totally?"

"Totally."

They swam in circles around their small piece of lake. He kept an ear out in case anyone thought to venture further down. This wasn't as high above the lake so you couldn't jump in from a great distance.

When they both started to get wrinkly, they jumped out. Once they were dry, he made Grace sit while he put sunscreen on her body. The swimsuit was very conservative, but he wasn't going to complain. If anyone stumbled upon them, the last thing he wanted was for them to get a look at his woman.

With Grace, Drake didn't like sharing. She was all his, and he wasn't about to share her with anyone.

Grace unpacked the picnic, and he served them both up some pasta and cold grilled chicken. She was a damn good cook.

Once their food was finished, Grace teased him with chocolate cake, until he pinned her down, taking a piece for himself. After all the food was finished, he packed up the basket, and Grace lay between his thighs, and read from the e-reader he'd given to her. Drake laughed at some of the scenes she read out, and grew hot at a couple of the sex scenes.

"Did you purposefully fill this e-reader with porn?"

"It's not porn, and yes, I did."

"Why?"

"You're reading something that I had given you. I figured the more you read, the hotter you would get, and you would think about me as you did."

"So you did it on purpose?" Grace asked.

"From the moment I first saw you at the diner, I knew I wanted you."

"You did?"

"I did." He ran the tips of his fingers down her arms before wrapping them around her waist. "What do you think to that?"

"I had no idea. You settled for being my friend."

"I settled for what I could get, and you were only

ready to be friends."

Grace snuggled against him. "I'm pleased we're more. You know there are times I feel like we've been friends all of my life."

Drake tensed up as he heard a twig snap. Getting to his feet, he stood in front of Grace, protecting her.

A large man wearing a Trojans MC leather cut appeared. The man's hair was to his shoulders, and he was frowning.

"What are you doing here?" he asked.

"Just came to enjoy the view."

"You think I don't know another MC when I see one?"

"I'm not wearing my cut," Drake said.

"Then cover your fucking ink."

Looking down at his chest, he saw the MC emblem on display. It was small, but anyone who knew the Dirty Fuckers would recognize it. Drake grabbed his shirt, tugging it on.

"You're not here to start a war?"

"No. The name's Drake."

"I'm Knuckles." He looked past him to Grace. "Your old lady or club whore?"

"Old lady," Drake said. "We were just enjoying the water, and the sun. We stayed away from the town, and we won't stay long."

"Would you like us to leave?" Grace asked, standing up.

Knuckles looked from Drake to Grace.

"Dirty Fuckers are not known for causing trouble. Stick to your spot, and stay away from town. Duke will be in touch with James to let him know he gave you safe passage. Next time, phone ahead. We may even accept you at the clubhouse."

Drake thanked him. "I didn't come as a club

member, just as a man."

"Duly noted. Take care."

Knuckles turned his back, walking away, whistling.

"Is it always like that?" Grace asked.

"Not always. With clubs there can be a lot of tension. There's a lot of MCs, and quite a few of them fight over turf. Trojans are one of the most feared, but respect them, and they'll respect you."

"Did you disrespect them?"

Drake shook his head. "No. I didn't have my leather cut, nor did I have my bike. All I had was the ink I got when I joined the club. He wouldn't have known if that wasn't on show. It also helped that I stayed to my side of town. I didn't try to push my way through town."

"I think it's time we go."

He didn't argue, and they packed away their stuff.

Grace flung herself into his arms, and he pressed her against the nearest tree. "I don't want to go just yet."

Unable to resist, he moved her costume to one side, shoved his boxer shorts down, and slammed deep inside her. He didn't bag his cock up, but he didn't see the point. He may have already gotten her pregnant.

****

Friday night

"It's not scary," Teri said.

"That's easy for you to say. You've been to a lot of them."

"I live for them. You do know the parties are every single night. Drake only suggested Friday night because you're not working tomorrow."

"I didn't know that." Grace looked out of the diner. "Every single night?"

"If the guys want to party, they drink some beer, eat, and fuck all they want." Teri popped some gum and finished wiping down the counters. There was a large pot of soup simmering on the stove.

It was still summer, and Teri was experimenting with soup.

"What is up with that?" Grace asked, pointing at the large pot.

"Fall will be here before you know it, and I like to get ahead. I'm simmering some chicken carcasses to make my own stock. Once that is done, I can use the stock to experiment on other soups, and it would be an awesome base. Chicken, vegetable, even Chinese soups."

Grace loved Teri's enthusiasm.

"Also, there's no point throwing out the chicken when it's perfectly good, and it tastes amazing." Teri popped some gum. "While you wait for Drake, you could chop me up these vegetables."

Grabbing a knife, Grace got to work prepping the vegetables, and watching as Teri pulled out fresh herbs and then a variety of spices. The woman knew how to work wonders in the kitchen, and Grace loved watching.

"So, you and Drake, he's told me that you've accepted being his old lady."

"He wanted to go to the party tonight, and make sure that I was ready to be his old lady." Grace shrugged. "I love being with him."

"I see that smile on your face, babe. You're in love."

Grace paused. "Love?"

"Yes. You're in love with Drake."

"I think that's a little too soon, don't you?"

"Not really. It's just the right time."

"Dwayne?"

"Is your ex, and he's completely out of the picture."

He *was* totally out of the picture. She'd not even

given him a thought until that moment. Drake made her forget about the past, and look forward to the now, and the future.

"Wow, love, that's a pretty big deal."

"And if I'm not wrong, Drake's also mega in love with you, like totally, mega in love. I've never seen him look so damn happy." Teri kept on talking while Grace was having a semi-nervous breakdown.

It was possible to fall in love in such a short period of time? Most loves were the kind that people spent years building.

"Hey, baby, are you ready?" Drake asked. He held up a paper bag that had the label of Suzy's work place.

"Go on, honey. You can use my office to get changed."

Grace really wished that Teri hadn't dropped that bombshell, as otherwise she'd be able to focus a hell of a lot more right now. She felt out of sorts, and not ready to spend the evening with Drake.

"Is everything okay?" Drake asked when she was close to him.

"Of course, why wouldn't I be?"

He reached out, stroking her cheek. "No reason, you just look a little put out. Has someone said anything?"

"No. I'm happy. I'm nervous. I've never been to a real party before, not even when I was at college."

She smiled at him, hoping to hide the turmoil going through her mind.

Love?

"I'll be there with you. You've got nothing to be afraid of."

"This is what you want me to wear?" she asked, taking the bag.

"Yes. It's the right size as well."

"Your ego is showing."

"I know your size." He kissed her head. "Would you like me to come in with you?" he asked, winking.

"I'm good. You'll get to see the end result." She kissed his cheek, leaving him in the kitchen, and making her way into Teri's office.

Closing the door, she flicked the lock in case someone entered. Sitting down in Teri's chair, she leaned forward putting her head in her hands. What the hell was happening with her?

"Just get dressed, go to the party, and pretend this is not happening."

It all sounded so easy in her head.

Opening the bag, she started looking through the clothes. She found a short skirt, and an even shorter top. What the hell?

She remembered the women hanging out with the Dirty Fuckers, and the way they had spoken to her.

"Fuck it."

It was the short skirt, or spending the night alone.

Doubts rushed through her head, but instead of forgetting about the night with Drake, she stood, removed her clothing, and put on the clothes he'd picked out. Once she was done, she stood in front of the mirror that Teri had in her office. Grace wondered if the reason Teri had one in her office was so that she was ready for the parties.

Again, Grace pushed the thoughts aside, and tugged her hair up on top of her head, pulling it together with a band.

She didn't have any makeup, and she'd never really been a fan. Licking her lips, she opened the door, and forced a smile. "What do you think?"

Drake stared up and down the length of her body.

"Fuck me, baby." He moved in close, gripping her ass. "I want to fuck you so badly." He slammed his lips down on hers, and the moment he touched her, Grace got the feeling that everything was going to be okay in the world. She had nothing to be afraid of.

"Take me to your party," she said.

"Every guy there is going to want to get you naked."

"You're causing a scene," Teri said.

Grace jerked out of Drake's arms, her cheeks heating. She'd completely forgotten where she was, and that had never happened to her before.

"Doesn't my woman look hot?" Drake asked.

Rolling her eyes, she smiled at Teri. She really did like her boss.

"I'd fuck you, honey."

"What?" Grace asked, not sure if she had heard correctly. There was no way her boss had just said that, was there?

"Baby, I swing whichever way the pleasure is coming from. I love it anyway I can get it." Teri gave her a hug. "Have fun tonight. Give the club a chance, and if you're still around after I finish here, I'll have a drink with you."

Teri left them alone, and Drake took her hand, leading her out of the diner.

"Are we taking your bike?" Grace asked.

"Not a chance. We're going to take the time to walk up to the clubhouse." He pointed up a slight incline, and she saw the lights from the house, which looked a good ten minutes away. "We're going to talk."

"Talk?"

"You look terrified, and I'm going to calm your fears, and promise you that you've got nothing to be afraid of."

Does he have feelings for me?

"I have a question," she said.

"I'm listening."

"Where do you see us going?"

"What do you mean?"

"Am I some summer fun?"

Drake started laughing. "Honey, we're not high school teenagers. I passed the stage for a summer romance over twenty years ago." He paused, gripped the back of her neck, and tilted her head back so she had no choice but to look at him. "With you, it's the real deal, babe."

"Real deal. I don't know what that is."

He leaned in, taking possession of her lips, and she closed her eyes, enjoying the feel of his kiss. "It means that I'm not using you. This is not some fleeting romance. This is it for me. I want to wake up next to you, have breakfast, and even take that little ball of fluff you call a dog for walks. I want to get to know you, to find out what makes you tick." He sighed, running his thumb against her lip. "I get a rush just being around you. Don't you feel it?"

"I do."

"What's the matter, Grace?"

"I don't know. I'm scared."

Drake cupped her face with both of his hands. "You've got nothing to be afraid of. From here on out, I'll take care of you. I'll make sure nothing ever happens to you that will cause you pain or hurt. I'm your man."

Tears filled her eyes. "This is all kind of surreal. You're a biker."

"And you're a waitress." He kissed her lips, and she gripped him tightly. "Now, my waitress, my old lady, let's go and enjoy the party."

****

MY KIND OF DIRTY

Suzy watched as Chloe finished getting dressed for the party. It had been a few weeks since Chloe had been to a club party. This was the first night she was going to be alone.

"You can come if you want to," Chloe said. "There's always plenty of men to go around."

"Nah, I'm going to keep my virgin ass on this sofa with Fluff, and we're going to watch a movie."

"What kind of movie?" Chloe asked.

"The romantic kind, I think. I'm in the mood for a little romance."

"Well, if you change your mind give me a call, and I can make sure you don't leave the club a virgin."

Suzy chuckled. "Great, my roommate selling my virginity to a bunch of bikers."

"Not selling, honey. They'd be taking it for free. They don't pay for pussy. Besides, I'm supposed to be your friend as well."

"You are. I'm sorry, I'm just tired. I'm going to enjoy a night in, relaxing."

"If you're sure?"

Suzy nodded. "More than sure."

Ten minutes later, she was alone, and wondering why she didn't just go to the damn party. Pushing her thoughts aside, she loaded up the movie, and sat eating a large bag of cheesy chips with Fluffy curled up against her.

"Love is for suckers, Fluff. You're the only guy I need in my life." She gave his chin a little stroke, then went back to watching her movie.

The movie ended, and she was about to load another when a knock sounded at her door.

Frowning, she moved across the room, and checked through the peephole, surprised by who was there.

Opening the door, she stared at Pixie. "How do you know where I live?"

"I know where Chloe lives. She's club property, even if she doesn't believe it."

Before she could stop him, he'd already moved into her apartment, and Suzy had no choice but to close the door.

"I don't know why you're here. Chloe is out, and so is Grace. I really don—" Pixie slammed her against the wall and took possession of her mouth, silencing any kind of protest she once had.

His tongue glided across her bottom lip, and Suzy was too weak to deny him.

Opening her lips, she closed her eyes, basking in the feel of him. Pixie felt a lot better under her hands than she ever imagined he would.

Suddenly, he pulled away but only to take hold of her hands, and press them above her head. "So, this is how it's going to go. I'm going to fuck you, and you're going to love every second of it. Neither of us are going to speak a word of this with anyone, and we're going to keep doing this."

"You can't speak a word of it."

"I just said that, didn't I?"

"You're an asshole."

"And you're a fucking prude, but I'm sick and tired of you pushing me away. That shit stops now."

"Whatever." Suzy wondered if she should tell him she was a virgin or to let it go.

When he tugged her shirt over her head, Suzy decided it wouldn't hurt all that much. Women had been doing it for centuries, and surviving it. She'd survive it.

Chapter Eleven

Sitting at one of the tables, Grace stared around the room and had to wonder if she had walked into an orgy. There was more tit and cock than she ever thought was possible. Nothing could have prepared her for this.

Drake had bought her a beer, which had gone undrunk at the table. Biting her lip, she glanced to the left of her, and she quickly averted her eyes. A woman was bent over showing her ass off, and she was sucking a man's cock. That wouldn't have been a problem if there hadn't been a man behind her, preparing her asshole.

"I don't know where to look," Grace said.

His arm went around her shoulders, and he leaned down, turning her head so that she was looking at the woman's ass once again. "Look at whatever you want. If they didn't want you to watch, they wouldn't be here, and they'd be in their private room."

Grace watched as the man pressed his finger into the woman's ass. He pumped inside her ass, and then added a second finger, making sure that she was good and slick for his cock. They turned the woman so that she had a good view of him sliding his cock inside her. The man's cock was gloved up, and she watched in fascination as the woman's ass seemed to suck the guy's dick inside her.

"She wants it bad, baby." Drake turned her head, and tilted her head back. "You ever been taken in the ass?"

She shook her head. Words seemed really difficult to come by.

"Would you like to try it?"

"Wouldn't it hurt?"

"Not if it's done right, it wouldn't." He pressed another kiss to her lips, and stroked her cheek. "Come on, grab your beer, and let's go for a walk."

With a beer in hand, Grace watched the room as they were all in different states of fucking. Grace didn't know where to look. She wasn't used to seeing everything being so graphic.

"This happens every Friday?" Grace asked.

"This happens every single day, baby."

"You're surrounded by this all the time?"

"No, I come to you, baby. This is every day, and normal to me. You're the person I want the most, and I come to you. We're exclusive."

Grace smiled. They moved outside, and the action hadn't stopped there. She saw another guy leaning against the wall getting his dick sucked, while playing with another woman's pussy, as he sucked on a tit.

Drake tucked her under his arm. "When I see this, all I want to do is be balls deep inside you." He nibbled her neck, sucking on her ear. "Fuck, baby, I want to be inside you so bad." Drake moved her so that she was standing in front of him, and he wrapped his arms around her stomach, moving on underneath her shirt, cupping her tit. The other he moved down to cup her pussy so that he was full of her. She was going to fight him but decided against it. This was what she wanted as much as he did. "You're soaking wet."

"I know."

"Do you like watching?"

"Yes, but I don't want them to touch."

"I wouldn't let anyone else touch what belongs to me." He sucked her neck, biting down on her neck.

She took a swig of her beer as he fingered her clit, moving down to plunge inside her. She swallowed the beer, closing her eyes as he pinched her clit before sliding down to fuck inside her.

Opening her eyes, she saw that several men were

looking at her. With Drake's arms wrapped around her, she didn't care.

"None of these men will touch you because they know you belong to me. You're free to show what I do to you, and to know they're jealous as fuck that I've got you, and they don't have a clue how damn good you are. *I* know. I know how tight and wet your cunt gets. I know how greedy you are for my cum."

"Drake, we've got to talk about that," she said, trying to remember that she had to talk to him about their unprotected sex. She'd never been on the pill, and had been so stupid to not even think about it.

"I want you to get pregnant, Grace. I really want to put my baby inside you."

His words surprised and delighted her.

"You want to have kids?"

"I want kids, and I want to spend the rest of my life with you." He kissed her neck. "What do you say, Grace? Are you willing to take the leap with me?"

"Drake, I don't know, what are you saying?"

He pulled his hands out of her panties and from her bra, going down on one knee. "I'm saying, baby, will you marry me?"

What the hell?

Before she could even think about it, she smiled. "Yes, yes, I'll marry you."

He whooped and picked her up. Grace didn't even think, all she did was feel, and held onto Drake as he carried her back through the house toward his bedroom.

"She's going to marry me," he said, shouting it out for everyone to hear.

Grace hid her face against his shoulder, trying to calm her nerves.

What have I done?

Holding on tightly to him, she squealed as he dumped her on the bed, slamming the door closed.

"What are you doing, Drake?" she asked, giggling.

"I need to be inside you." He tugged his jeans down, pushing her skirt up, and tearing her panties off her body.

Her pussy grew slick, and she started to fight to get her clothes off. Drake helped, tearing the new clothes that he'd bought. By the time he slid inside her, they were both laughing.

"Fuck, baby, I don't care how it happens, I want to be inside you." He groaned. He sucked on her nipples, biting down hard.

"Yes, yes, yes, yes," she said, tightening around his rock hard cock.

He reached between them and started to stroke her clit, and Grace couldn't hold off her orgasm any longer. Drake pounded inside her, and she came around his cock, loving how hot and hard he was.

"That's it, baby, fuck, yes." He groaned, and she felt the pulse of his cock as he spilled inside her.

****

The following morning, Grace sneaked out of Drake's bedroom wearing a pair of his boxer briefs and one of his long shirts. She was surprised they actually fit, but she needed to get away from him right now. Tucking her hair behind her ears, she grabbed her pumps, and closed the door silently before heading downstairs. She passed a woman who was sleeping naked against the stairs with a man between her thighs.

It wasn't the nicest sight in the world. She left the clubhouse without too many people stopping her. Last night had been amazing, scary, and fucking wonderful. Drake had asked her to marry him, and she had said yes.

Only now, she was starting to wonder what the fuck she was doing.

You're in love with him.

Being in love and getting married were a long way away. They had only been having sex for a few weeks, and now she could be pregnant.

On the way down the long path, she paused when she caught sight of Pixie walking toward her.

"Morning," Pixie said, whistling.

"You're in a good mood."

"Yes. I am."

Grace frowned. "Why?"

"It's none of your business, but don't you worry, you're not going to put me in a bad mood."

She watched as he continued to whistle and make his way back toward the clubhouse. Shaking her head, she made her way into the diner, letting herself into the back door. Teri was already there, drinking a coffee.

"Morning," Grace said. "Did you put Pixie in a good mood?"

"I've not seen Pixie since he left the clubhouse last night. Fuck, my head is pounding, and I feel like I'm going to throw up." Teri dropped her head into her arms. "This is the first time that I don't think I'm going to be able to cook."

Grace tapped Teri's shoulder, and the woman turned to look at her.

"What the hell are you wearing?"

"I sneaked out of Drake's room."

"I heard you're getting married. Congratulations."

Moving away from her friend, Grace went into the changing room, and started to put her spare uniform on.

"Why do I get the feelings there's something I don't know?" Teri asked, entering the room, and closing the door.

Pinning her hair up, Grace shook her head. "There's nothing to say. Honestly."

"Every other woman getting married would be screaming from the rooftops, and you look like it's the worst news you've ever heard."

"It's not the worst news."

"Wait, hold up, you're not excited about getting married?" Teri asked. "Please speak quietly. My head has several men slamming my brain with sledgehammers."

"I don't know what I am." Grace closed her locker.

"You're not excited."

"I'm … I don't know."

"You accepted his marriage proposal last night."

"I know I did, and I did so in good faith that I wanted to get married."

"And now?" Teri asked.

"It's too soon. I may be pregnant, and he wants me to be pregnant. This kind of thing, it ruins relationships, and I don't want to be a regret."

She pushed past Teri and started to place the new menus on each table. All the time she was aware of Teri following her.

"You can't break up with him," Teri said.

"I'm not going to break up with him. I love him." She slapped her hand across her mouth, and stared at Teri.

Teri clapped her hands, chuckling, and then grabbing her head at the sudden pain. "Fuck. I don't think I can cook today."

"I can cook for you. If you're really worried, you can sit and assist?"

"I shouldn't have drunk all that tequila I did last

night. It was a night of partying, and I loved every single second of it."

Grace smiled. "I can help."

"I'll call Chloe and see if she can take your shift while you cook for me."

She watched Teri leave the room.

Letting out a sigh, Grace sat down on the bench and put her head into her hands. In that moment she thought about Dwayne. He'd never made her feel anything like Drake did. She loved Drake, and she'd never loved Dwayne.

When her thoughts didn't settle down, she got to her feet, and made her way into the kitchen where Teri was hanging up the phone. "Chloe's on her way in."

"Great," Grace said, clapping her hands together. "Let's get started."

For the next hour, she followed Teri's instructions, and started firing up the breakfast menu. Chloe entered half an hour into the preparations, and she got the congratulations to which she smiled.

What is your problem?
You love Drake.
You want to marry him.

She was scared. That was it. She was scared of making that final commitment. From in the kitchen, Grace heard the ring of the bell, and glanced over at Teri. "It's all about to begin. Are you ready for this?"

"I've got no choice. How is that head?"

"I'll be fine just as soon as the throbbing ends." Teri sipped at some water, and the first order rang through.

Showtime.

****

Drake walked into the diner to see Teri and Chloe serving with no sign of Grace. Her torn up clothing was still on his bedroom floor, but there wasn't a sign of his woman. Teri waved at him before making her way over.

"What's wrong?" he asked. "Why are you not cooking?"

"Can we take this outside?" Teri said.

He nodded, and they made their way out of the diner into the open warm air.

"What's going on?"

"Grace is cooking for me. I was too ill to even use the ovens today. I'd have ended up burning myself before I actually achieved anything." Teri dropped her sunglasses over her eyes. "So, you've proposed to Grace."

"Yeah, but I'm a little concerned right now. She sneaked out of my bedroom, and there's no sign of the woman I took to bed last night."

"She's having second thoughts," Teri said.

"About my proposal?"

Teri nodded her head. "Grace is a delicate kind of flower. She just doesn't jump into shit, and she is scared."

"Fuck. Let me go and talk to her."

"Can I give you a little bit of advice?" Teri asked.

"Yes!" He'd had no intention of proposing marriage to her. Last night, he'd just done what felt right, and he didn't want to make Grace scared of herself.

"Take your time with her. Don't rush her, and give her the space she needs."

He started to pace up and down and faced her. "Do you want me to leave her?"

"No. Just don't crowd her. Give her a chance to breathe."

"I'm not squashing her."

"You are by constantly surrounding her." Teri grabbed his hand. "You're a good man. I know this. You know this, but you also need to see that relationships take time. Grace is not like that whore who gave you herpes. She's not like the women who are fucking you for a leather cut and a title. Grace enjoys being around you. I've seen the way she has developed just by being with you. She cares about you, and is probably the only woman who will ever love you for you."

"Charming," he said. "And it wasn't herpes, it was gonorrhea."

"Whatever. You know I love you, and the club loves you, but this isn't about that kind of love. This is about the kind of love that will last a lifetime. Now, I didn't think it was ever going to be possible to love someone like that, but you have proven me wrong. That kind of love exists. I see it in the way you look at Grace, the way she looks at you."

"I'll take my time." He grabbed her arms. "I know Grace, okay. She may not think I do, but I know my woman, and Grace is scared because she thinks something is going to change. She's probably wondering what the hell we're going to do, but have a little faith that I won't go crazy."

He kissed Teri's head and made his way back into the diner. Entering the kitchen, he watched Grace stirring a pot of blueberry sauce.

"Hey, baby," he said, moving toward her.

Grace glanced over her shoulder, and she smiled at him. "Hey."

Drake saw the concern in her eyes, the fear.

"So, I woke this morning to find my woman had left my bed."

"I had to come to the diner early, and I didn't want to wake you."

He moved behind her, gripping her shoulders. Kissing her neck, he nibbled on her pulse. "You've got nothing to be afraid of. Nothing is going to change."

"You don't know that."

"I do know that, baby. I know everything." He wrapped his arms around her waist, pressing his cock against her ass. "Now, you may think I'm going to demand shit of you, but nothing is going to change. If you want, I won't even get you a ring if you're not ready."

"Do you think I'm crazy?"

"Of course. You're completely crazy, but you know what, I wouldn't have you any other way." He turned her to face him, and he cupped her face.

"Do you hate me?"

"I don't hate you."

"Most women would be so damn happy right now, and I am, but I'm just … I don't know."

"You're having doubts."

"We don't really know each other."

"We know each other, but that's okay, I can wait." He kissed her head, breathing her scent in. "I'm going to let you cook, and do your thing. I'll see you later."

****

Later that night Grace was curled up on the sofa with Chloe on the floor, and Suzy holding her feet.

"Why are you here and not with your man?" Suzy asked.

She glanced down staring at the luminous pink nail polish that Suzy was putting on her toes.

"I wanted to spend a girly night." She rested her head on the sofa.

"You've become engaged, and you're having a girly night instead of screwing your man's brains out?" Chloe asked. "That is messed up."

"It's not."

"It is," Suzy said. "If I had a guy I'd be at home with him."

Grace rolled her eyes. "You don't even know what you're missing out on."

Suzy opened her mouth, and smiled. "Yeah, you're right."

"If I was getting married to the guy, I'd be with him so no other bitch would take what belonged to me. I guess we're all different."

"You think I'm doing the wrong thing?" Grace asked.

"I don't think anything," Chloe said. "We're two different people."

"I'm scared. The only other relationship I've been in was with Dwayne, and you both know how that turned out."

"First, Dwayne was a loser, and you shouldn't be putting Drake in the same category as him," Chloe said.

"I'm not."

"You totally are," Suzy said.

"Okay, what about the club?" Grace asked. "There are always willing women around them."

"Relationships are based on love and trust. If you don't love Drake, then trust is never going to come into it," Chloe said.

"I'm in love with Drake."

"But do you trust him? Has he done anything to make you think otherwise?"

Grace shook her head. She was being a complete and total idiot. "He's the one. I'm in love with him."

Chloe and Suzy screamed. "We knew it. We knew you were in love with him. Now, you just got to stop being afraid, and realize you've got a hot piece of ass who wants your hot piece of ass. If another woman comes sniffing around, stand up, tell her to back the fuck off, or you're going to bitch slap her."

Grace laughed. "I've been a bitch, haven't I?

"Yep, so stop being a bitch, and let things happen. Stop being afraid of what *could* happen, and enjoy what is actually happening. Come on, let's dance." Chloe jumped up, and turned on the radio. "It's time to party."

Music filled the apartment, and it was exactly what Grace needed. She threw her hands in the air, and screamed out happily.

"I'm going to get married."

In that moment, Grace didn't know why, but everything just seemed to come together in her mind. She was going to get married to Drake, a member of the Dirty Fuckers MC, and she was in love with him.

Chapter Twelve

Three weeks later

Chloe was humming to herself as she cleaned away the table that the family had just vacated. Everything in her life was going great. She now had Grace's room in the apartment. Grace had moved into the clubhouse, and was currently looking for a house or apartment with Drake. There were also all the plans of the wedding. Teri was baking up a storm in the kitchen, and with fall almost upon them, things were slowing down in the diner so there was more than enough time for Teri to bake. Grace had asked for Teri to bake her wedding cake.

Drake and Grace sat in the corner of the diner looking through wedding magazines. Grace wanted a church wedding, and Chloe was so damn happy as she'd been asked to be a bridesmaid.

Whistling to herself, she carried the plates into the kitchen, handing them to Daniel. The young man was still prospecting for the club, and was doing a good job. Chloe hadn't gone back to the club apart from that one party three weeks ago. She hadn't even slept with anyone that night either.

The club was changing, and more men were finding women of their own while she was left out in the cold. The man she wanted, she couldn't have. It had been a long time since she'd seen Richard, and many of her nights were spent thinking about him. Even when she promised herself she wouldn't give him a thought, she always did.

"Hey, Chloe," Richard said, appearing as if he'd been reading her very thoughts. Spinning around, she saw him standing there, holding a briefcase.

"Richard, what are you doing here?" she asked.

"I wanted to see you."

"Why?" She stared at him dressed in his business suit looking rather dashing. Arousal hit her instantly at the sight of him. He looked so handsome and sexy, and she knew exactly what those clothes hid.

Get a hold of yourself.

"I want to ask you out on a date."

She stood up, giving Richard her full attention.

"I'm not sure I heard that properly."

"You heard me properly." Richard sighed. "I want to go on a date with you. I want to be with you, and get to know you."

"You're asking me out on a date?"

"Yes. I'm asking you out on a date, and it's not to come to the diner. There's this sweet little French restaurant, and I'd love for you to come with me."

Chloe's heart pounded as she stared at him. "A date."

"Yes. I will pick you up around seven, and we'll have some dinner, maybe go dancing, and then I'll take you home afterward."

"A proper date?"

"A proper date with no expectations." He held his hand out. "I miss you, Chloe, and not just the sex. I miss you."

Chloe stared down at his hand, and the temptation to put her hand in his was so strong. She kept her hands to herself. "I will accept your date. I won't be fucking you or anything."

Richard laughed. "I figured I'd have to work up to actually being with you."

"Will you be coming to Drake and Grace's wedding?" Chloe asked, needing to get onto a topic that actually made sense.

"Yes. I've been invited. That was something else I wanted to ask you. Will you be my date to the wedding?" he asked.

"Wow, when it rains it pours." Blowing out a breath, she ran her hand down the front of her uniform. Glancing down, she saw that there was a tomato ketchup stain, mustard, and even a coffee stain. She had to look the most unattractive she ever had in her life, and yet Richard was asking her out, not once, but twice. "Yes, I will be your date."

There. She had done it.

Richard nodded. "I will see you at seven, and I'll send a dress."

"You'll send a dress?" she asked.

"I want you to feel like the most beautiful woman in the world."

"Okay, then I will accept."

****

"So, our friends are having this big thing going on."

Suzy turned around to find Pixie standing in the back of the shop while she was going through orders. "What are you doing here? The shop isn't even open." She had to close due to the delivery, and several colleagues had phoned in sick. Most of the time Suzy was more than happy to watch the shop, and deal with the deliveries all on her own, but they were going through a season change. The extra help would have been appreciated. In the end, she'd had to close the doors to go through the supplies.

"You left your keys in my car?" He held her spare keys between his fingers, and heat filled her cheeks. The one night they were supposed to have spent together hadn't exactly worked out as she planned. Pixie seemed to touch buttons she didn't even realize that she possessed.

"You should have given them to me." She took them back and stepped away from him.

"What's wrong, my little virgin? Are you afraid?"

"Stop it." When it came to Pixie, she was weak. He said all the right things, and made her want everything that she had once denied herself. Pixie was her addiction, and worse, he knew it. Three weeks she'd been sneaking around with him, and yet no one even had a clue that they were fucking every chance they got.

"Stop what? Stop tempting you? Stop teasing you?" He walked up behind her, gripping her neck, and tilting her head back. His lips covered hers in a searing kiss that had her pussy getting wet. "Stop making you so wet that you want to be fucked so hard?"

She pushed away from him, not having a clue where she found the strength.

"What do you want?"

"Do you want to go to Drake and Grace's wedding with me?"

Suzy stared at him. "Why would we do that?"

"We're fucking, Suzy. It's only a matter of time before someone finds out."

"Yet no one knows. Why ruin something that is working for us? Besides, there's probably plenty of club women there."

"I'm not fucking club women, Suzy."

"What?"

"I've not touched any other woman but you since that first night. I want you to go to the wedding with me."

Suzy was speechless. "I don't want to ruin what we've got."

"How is going to a wedding going to ruin that?"

She rubbed her temple. "I don't know."

"Then go with me."
In that moment, she was tempted.

****

Grace wiped down the table in the clubhouse and pushed some hair off her face. She had gotten off work an hour ago and already cleaning. So far she and Drake hadn't found anywhere to stay, which sucked. She didn't want to stay at the clubhouse forever.

"You could leave it," Cora said, coming downstairs looking like she had spent the whole morning fucking.

"I can't leave it. Look, it's a mess."

"James would make the guys clean it. He's not one for too much mess, or he'd hire one of those firms. You know the ones that clean." Cora moved toward the kettle. "How are the wedding plans going?"

"Good, I think. Drake wants to have the wedding in the yard of the clubhouse."

"Where do you want it?"

"In the church. I always wanted to get married in white, and in a church. You know, the traditional stuff?"

"He doesn't want that?" Cora asked.

Grace shook his head. "He said it would be bad for his biker image."

Cora burst out laughing. "Honey, tell him blue balls wouldn't be good for his image. This is your wedding as much as his."

"So?"

"So, compromise. Find something that he'll want more than the wedding in the backyard, or forfeit sex." Cora took a sip of her coffee. "You'll come to see there are ways for us to win. Just think it over." She glanced down at her watch. "I've got to go. I'm helping Sharon out at the school."

"Wait, Cora," Grace said, stopping the other

woman. "Suzy has agreed to be my maid of honor, and Chloe is going to be my bridesmaid. Would you also be a bridesmaid?"

Cora squealed, wrapping her arms around Grace. "I wouldn't miss it. Thank you so much for asking me."

Holding onto the other woman, Grace felt a lot happier for asking Cora. They were both old ladies in the club.

"Remember, compromise," Cora said, leaving her alone.

Taking a seat at the counter, Grace thought about what Drake wanted at the wedding. He wanted to be surrounded by his club, and the bikes, and she wanted to be in a church with the dress. Drake hadn't disputed the dress, even though she'd not been a virgin with him.

"Hey, baby," Drake said, startling her out of her thoughts.

She noticed several of the brothers walked into the clubhouse, giving her a nod of acknowledgement. Licking her suddenly dry lips, she took a deep breath. "I want to get married in a church." Drake groaned, and she held her hand up. "You've got to hear me out before you start complaining. You're hearing church and being ignorant. Now, I want to marry you because *you* asked me. I think I should get a say where we marry."

"A church? We'll burn entering the fucking place."

"I'll be willing to forgo the tux if you want to wear your leathers. Also, no limo, and we ride on your bike."

"The dress?" Drake asked.

"I'm going to be wearing a white dress, and only once. If it ends up dirty, I'll not be saving it."

"That's fucking extravagant."

"One expense, one church, and you get your

bikes, your club, and your leather. Please, please, please." She ran her hands up his chest, circling his neck. "I'll do that thing with my tongue you like."

"Fine, we'll get married in the church." He sank his fingers into her hair, slamming his lips down on hers.

Grace chuckled, kissing him back.

****

Drake rode into the city. His wedding was taking place in just over a week, and Grace was happier with the idea of a church wedding. None of his brothers were with him, and this was more out of curiosity than anything else.

He'd gotten the directions on the internet, and he parked up outside of the apartment building.

Parking his bike, he made his way inside the apartment, and saw the name he was looking for. Going upstairs, he knocked on the door, and waited. Tapping his keys against his thigh, he glanced up and down the clean corridor with three other apartments. There were two behind him, and one beside Grace's old apartment.

The door opened just slightly, and a woman's gaze stared back at him. She was already sporting a black eye, and Drake was happy that he'd come.

"Can I come in?"

"Er, no, I don't understand. I don't know you, and I've never seen you with Dwayne."

Drake smiled. "Dwayne and I go way back. We've got a friend in common."

"He'll get angry with me."

"He hits you and beats you. Look at you, you're terrified."

"It's all my fault," the woman said.

"No, it's not your fault." Drake reached into his jacket, pulling out the number of a local officer who dealt with domestic cases. He'd done his research before coming here.

Drake handed the card over, and she took it.

She opened the door, staring at the number. "He was so nice. When I first saw him, he was so sweet and loving. He always said it was my fault, and nothing I ever did was right."

"It's not your fault. This has been going on for what, a month, two months?" he asked.

"We've been together three months."

"Do you want to stay?" Drake asked.

"No, I want to get out."

"Pack your shit up, go to the cops, and press charges against him." Drake took a seat. "I'll be here to make sure he stays away. You can pack up, and be gone. I'll deal with Dwayne."

He watched the young woman rush around trying to pack everything she owned into one bag. There wasn't a lot, and before long she left the house.

"You're not coming as well?" she asked.

"Nope. I've got a bone to pick with him, and I'm going to sit right here until I speak with him." Drake lowered himself onto the sofa.

"He'll hurt you."

Drake laughed. "Don't worry, honey, I'm more than happy to get my ass kicked." He watched her leave, and then he waited. Grace didn't have a clue where he was, and he was going to keep it that way.

Two hours passed before the elusive Dwayne entered the apartment.

"Rosie, baby, I want you," Dwayne said, closing the door.

"Sorry, baby, no Rosie here," Drake said.

He watched as Dwayne spun around, glaring at him.

"Who the fuck are you?" Dwayne asked.

"Hello, Dwayne. I hear you have quite a bit of a temper on you."

"Has that bitch been talking? She's fucking lying. Rosie!"

"Rosie is gone, and I'm not talking about her, even though I bet that black eye speaks for itself."

"She walked into a door."

"A fist shaped door?"

"Can't prove nothing," Dwayne said. "Who'll believe her?"

Drake smiled. "Anyway, I'm not here about Rosie. I'm here about Grace."

He saw recognition in Drake's eyes, along with the shot of fear. "What about that whore?"

"That whore is going to be my wife, and I wanted to see what fucker thought he could put his hands on her in anger. Imagine my surprise I see you," Drake said, sneering at him.

Stepping forward, he wrapped his fingers around Dwayne's neck and slammed him up against the wall.

"Grace doesn't give a fuck about you, but I wanted to look the man who hurt her, in the eyes. I'm going to warn you, you come near Grace, you make any sign of trying to get back into her life, and I will fucking end you."

"I've not been near Grace."

"Let me get one thing straight. If I hear you've hurt any other woman, I'll come and find you, Dwayne. I don't like scum like you, men who beat women. You're not tough. You're a fucking wimp, a wuss, and men who raise a hand to a woman is not the kind of man I want breathing the same air as me." He squeezed the bastard's neck, wanting to end his life, but Drake had taken a vow. He'd vowed never to harm another living person unless he had to.

With Dwayne, he'd keep an eye on the fucker, and make sure he didn't harm another person ever again.

Slamming his fist into Dwayne's stomach, Drake stepped over him and left the apartment. On the way down to his bike, he put a call through to the officer whose number he'd given Rosie. He let the cop know that he'd given Dwayne a warning, and Drake was reassured that an eye would be kept on Dwayne.

Once that was done, he ended the call only to have his cell phone go off again. Seeing it was Grace, he answered with a smile.

"Hey, baby, what's up?"

"Are you going to be having a stripper?"

"A stripper? What the fuck for?"

"Your bachelor party."

"I don't know. James is in charge of all parties. Why?"

"Erm, well, Chloe's in charge of my bachelorette party."

"No. Not fucking happening. You're not having a fucking stripper male or female."

"It's not something I've organized. This is down to Chloe. You'll have to talk to her."

Before he could argue, Grace hung up, and he cursed.

He dialed Chloe's number, and waited.

"Hello," Chloe said.

"No stripper, nothing."

Chloe giggled. "I know you're going to be having a stripper, so I'm going to make sure that Grace gets something. This relationship will be equal."

Again, he was hung up on, and it pissed him off. Pocketing his cell phone, Drake didn't have a clue what he was going to do to stop a guy taking his clothes off in front of his woman, but he'd sure figure something out.

MY KIND OF DIRTY

Chapter Thirteen

Grace took a sip of her soda as the women started drinking. She didn't mind not having to drink as she couldn't wait to tell Drake the news. Glancing at her watch, she had to wonder if there was a stripper right now rubbing her body against Drake. She trusted Drake, and knew he wouldn't step out on her, but she couldn't help but feel jealous of it. Drake was hers. He belonged to her, and she didn't like the thought of sharing him, not one bit.

"I want to propose a toast," Chloe said, raising her glass. "To one of the nicest, sweetest, and craziest women I've ever known."

"I'll second that," Teri said. "Not many women would have taken Drake without some issues. You know, the herpes kind, or he calls it the gonorrhea kind."

She couldn't help but laugh. Drake had told her all about his gonorrhea problem, and what it had done to him, and how humiliated he was. Grace hadn't held it against him, although she'd found it particularly funny when his brothers teased him.

"What can I say? I love that man, and nothing is ever going to change that." She held onto her stomach, feeling protective of what she was growing. The start of their family, and she really wished she'd been able to tell him before the bachelor party, but there hadn't been any time.

The lights went down, and women screamed as suddenly the stage lit up, and Grace turned to see what it was. The moment she caught sight, she covered her mouth in shock and in laughter.

"They're completely crazy," she said.

"My man doesn't like the thought of me finding anyone else," Cora said, whistling up at the stage. Five men stood on the stage, and Grace glanced around the room to see the rest of the Dirty Fuckers were also in a similar state of undress.

Their backs were to them, and she saw their leather pants.

Suddenly, the center male spun around, and she saw Drake with a microphone.

"Hey, baby," he said, pointing at her. "So, I didn't want you to have a stripper, and there's only one woman I want to see naked, and that's you, honey. This is for you."

Music started up, and Grace didn't care about the other men. She only had eyes for her man, and she chuckled as all the men started to remove their clothes, swinging their hips, and teasing the crowd.

Cora rushed up to the stage, whistling at her man.

Grace stayed seated as she watched Drake move toward her but dance, removing clothes as he did.

"I wouldn't budge on the dancer," Chloe said, leaning in close. "This was the only thing I'd settle for."

"Where's Richard?" Grace asked.

"He's working tonight. Don't worry, this is your night, and I can see him at any time." Chloe patted her shoulder. "This is fun, right?"

"Right."

She turned her attention back to Drake only to find him a few feet away. Kissing Chloe's cheek, she made her way toward her man, wrapping her arms around his neck.

"Hey, baby," he said.

"Hey, Drake."

He started to dance with her, and she loved it.

"Are you having cold feet?"

"Not a chance. What about you? You're more likely to have cold feet than me?"

"I'd have been married to you already if you weren't so desperate to have a church wedding." He placed his hand on her butt, pulling her against him. She felt the hard length of his cock pressing against her stomach.

"There's something I want to talk to you about," she said. There was no point hiding what they had created together.

"What is it?" he asked.

"It's not something that you have to worry about. Well, it might be something you have to worry about, but I think that's expected with what we've done."

He cupped her face, forcing her to look at him. "I can't fix whatever problem you are having until you tell me what the problem is."

"I'm pregnant."

"What?"

"I'm pregnant." She looked down at her stomach. "We're going to have a baby."

Drake stared into her eyes then down at her stomach. "You're pregnant?"

"I'm pregnant."

"We're going to have a baby?" he asked.

She chuckled. "We're pregnant, and we're going to have a baby."

He screamed out, shouting from the top of his lungs the news.

Whistles, congrats rushed toward them, and she accepted them, loving Drake even more.

****

Grace didn't make him wear a tuxedo, and he married her within the church. Drake had to wonder if she was going to change her mind at the last minute, and he'd find a tux waiting. She stood beside him at the church, and they spoke their vows, promising to love each other. Drake would die for her, and he knew that his brothers would put their lives on the line to protect her. He'd do the same for his brothers and their women.

"You're fucking married. How did that fucking happen?" Caleb asked.

"I don't fucking know, man. I'm also going to be a father. I keep thinking I'm going to wake up." He sipped on a bottle of water. They were not staying at the clubhouse tonight. He was taking them to a hotel, and from there, they were going to the Caribbean for a couple of weeks.

Grace was only going to get bigger, and he wanted her to have a honeymoon to remember and to enjoy.

"What are you going to do about that one over there?" he said, pointing at Kitty Cat. Caleb's woman was standing with Cora, Stacey, Grace, Suzy, Lucy, Chloe, and Teri. Stacey had been allowed to come as she'd given an apology to Leo and Paul. It helped that Leo and Paul had gotten over Stacey, and were no longer giving her their attention. There were times he caught sight of Stacey staring at them, but again, she'd lost them both.

"There's nothing to do but wait. I start pushing, and she's going to run in the opposite direction. I've got to play it cool."

"Play it cool?"

"It's what I keep telling myself all the time. Play it cool, and Kitty will see I love her when she's damn good and ready."

Drake saw that Caleb was hurting.

"It will get easier."

"I've got no plans to leave her. I just wanted to wish you congratulations."

He shook Caleb's hands, and then moved toward

his wife. Grace was his wife. It seemed too crazy to even contemplate, but that was exactly what she was.

My wife.

Wrapping his arms around her waist, he tugged her against him, and they started dancing.

"Hello, husband."

"Hello, wife." He touched her back, moving around to stroke her stomach. "How's our kid?"

"Resting. *It* was kicking like crazy in the church."

Drake didn't care if it was a boy or girl. He only hoped that it was a healthy baby.

"This has been one of the best days of my life," Grace said. "I could never have imagined that day when I first saw you, us being here now."

"It has been quite a ride, don't you think? It's been hot, and dirty, and the stuff of dreams."

She giggled. "It really has, hasn't it? Wow, I still can't believe that we were friends, and then lovers."

"Nah, we fucked a hell of a lot. We just fucked each other with words, and our company."

Grace snorted. "I love you, Drake."

Kissing the top of her head, he held her close, refusing to let go.

"I love you, Grace. I will 'til the day I die, and then, if I can, I'll keep on loving you beyond that."

They danced for the rest of the night until it was time to go to the hotel. James shook his hand, giving him an envelope full of money, or at least, he thought it was money.

"What's this?"

"It's deeds to a house. I got Richard to start purchasing that one near the town. It has a little garden, and it's not far from Lucy and the kids. It's only little, but it's a start."

Drake was touched. "Grace will love it."

"When you get home, it will be fully furnished. Congratulations on the kid, and on your wife."

He hugged James, and then climbed into the back of the car. Drake handed the envelope to Grace.

"A house? He's got us a house?"

"It's what the club life means, baby."

"Oh my God, this is amazing."

Grace threw her arms around her, and Drake had to admit, he was just as touched.

MY KIND OF DIRTY

Epilogue

Nine months later

Grace sang to her son, putting little Joseph down for the night. Her son was such an angel to look after. He rarely cried unless he was hungry, and he slept through the night now. "You're the most beautiful thing I've ever seen," she said, stroking his cheek. "Tomorrow we're going to the clubhouse. Yeah, Aunty Cora is going to tell the whole club that she's pregnant. I don't know if Uncle James knows the news yet, but we're not going to miss it for the world."

"I bet he already knows," Drake said. She turned to find her husband leaning against the doorframe with his arms folded. "How is our little guy?"

"He's perfect, aren't you, baby?" she asked.

Drake gripped her neck as he stood beside her.

Joseph let out a baby squeal, lifting his arms up as if to be picked up.

"We shouldn't pick him up, should we?" Drake asked.

"I don't know. I mean, look at him, he's so sweet. What would it hurt?"

"Don't the books say that we have to be strong, and stick to a reasonable bedtime?" Drake asked.

They should probably leave him, but he was their son.

"One night won't be a problem," Grace said. "When have you ever followed the rules?"

Drake leaned down and picked him up. Together they moved toward the sofa, and Grace curled up on the arm of the chair with Drake between her thighs. He rested Joseph on his chest, and she leaned around and stroked her son's head. "He's so beautiful. Can you believe we made something that beautiful?"

"I can believe you made something this beautiful, Grace. Me, I don't." He took hold of her hand, locking their fingers together. "I love you, baby. Thank you for giving me a chance."

"We've been married a year, Drake, thank you."

It had been an amazing, wild, dirty, crazy year. Grace had no idea marriage could be so wonderful, and the more time she spent with Drake, the more she fell in love with him.

"Grace?" Drake said, whispering her name.

Joseph had settled into a spot and was slowly going to sleep. His eyes stayed closed for several seconds, and then grew heavy before going wide once again. She loved him so much.

"What?"

"I want to make another one."

"A baby?" she asked.

"Yes. He needs a brother or a sister."

"Well, when he's down for the night, we can get started on making another one." Grace climbed out from behind him, and when she was sure Joseph couldn't see her, she started to remove her clothes. "Come on, baby, we don't have all night."

She ran to their bedroom, collapsing to the bed, and opening her thighs.

Minutes passed, and she thought about climbing into bed, and getting some sleep.

Drake rounded the corner, his cock long, thick, and hard. He was completely naked.

"That, Grace, is a challenge I'm more than happy to accept."

He climbed on the bed, and proceeded to show her all night long exactly how many times he could fuck her.

MY KIND OF DIRTY

Grace loved every second of it. When they collapsed at the end of the night, Drake held her tightly against him, and she fell asleep, surrounded by his warmth, and his love.

The End

www.samcrescent.com

SAM CRESCENT

EVERNIGHT PUBLISHING ®

www.evernightpublishing.com

Printed in Great Britain
by Amazon